Abba! Was there ever another planet like that? With thirty thousand years of recorded history, the most exquisite etiquette, art and culture more refined and stylized than any other world—and its treatment of its women totally barbaric, monstrous, inhuman.

To Coyote Jones it was a complex puzzle in contradictions. On the one hand there was a murder plot against its most esteemed personage, Jacinth of the Seventh Level. On the other hand, because she was a woman she was virtually a prisoner of her station; her every achievement resulting in envious malice.

Coyote had to call upon the galactic Communipaths for information, on the planet's rulers for guidance, and finally upon the Chief of the Licensed Criminals for direction. *But ultimately he had to find his own way—if they didn't kill him and Jacinth first.*

At the
Seventh Level

SUZETTE HADEN ELGIN

DAW BOOKS, INC.
DONALD A. WOLLHEIM, PUBLISHER

1301 Avenue of the Americas
New York, N. Y.   10019

Copyright ©, 1972, by Suzette Hayden Elgin

For the Sake of Grace, copyright © 1969 by Mercury Press, Inc.

ALL RIGHTS RESERVED

COVER PAINTING AND ILLUSTRATIONS BY GEORGE BARR.

PRINTED IN U.S.A.

AT THE SEVENTH LEVEL

Prologue:

FOR THE LOVE OF GRACE   7

Interlude:

THE ROLL OF IAMBS AND THE CLANG OF SPONDEES   33

Novel:

ABBA   43

Epilogue:

MODULATION IN ALL THINGS   127

Prologue

FOR THE SAKE OF GRACE

The Khadilh ban-harihn frowned at the disk he held in his hand, annoyed and apprehensive. There was always, of course, the chance of malfunction in the com-system. He reached forward and punched the transmit button again with one thumb, and the machine clicked to itself fitfully and delivered another disk in the message tray. He picked it up, looked at it and swore a round assortment of colorful oaths, since no women were present.

There on the left was the matrix-mark that identified his family, the ban-harihn symbol quite clear; no possibility of error there. And from it curled the suitable number of small lines, yellow for the females, green for the males, one for each member of his household, all decorously in order. Except for one.

The yellow line that represented at all times the state of being of his wife, the Khadilha Althea, was definitely not as it should have been. It was interrupted at quarter-inch intervals by a small black dot, indicating that all was not well with the Khadilha. And the symbol at the end of the line was not the blue cross that would have classified the difficulty as purely physical; it was the indeterminate red star indicating only that the problem, whatever it was, could be looked upon as serious or about to become serious.

The Khadilh sighed. That would mean anything, from his wife's misuse of their credit cards through a security leak by one of her servants to an unsuitable love affair—

although his own knowledge of the Khadilha's chilly nature made him consider the last highly unlikely. The only possible course for him was to ask for an immediate full report.

And just what, he wondered, would he do, if the report were to make it clear that he was needed at home at once? One did not simply pick up one's gear and tootle off home from the outposts of the Federation. It would take him at the very least nine months to arrive in his home city-cluster, even if he were able to command a priority flight with suspended-animation berths and warp facilities. Damn the woman anyway, what could she be up to?

He punched the button for voice transmittal, and the com-system began to hum at him, indicating readiness for dialing. He dialed, carefully selecting the planet code, since his last attempt to contact his home, on his wife's birthday, had resulted in a most embarrassing conversation with a squirmy-tentacled creature that he had gotten out of its (presumed) bed in the middle of its (presumed) sleep. And he'd had to pay in full for the call, too, all intergalactic communication being on a buyer-risk basis.

". . . three-three-two-three-two . . ." he finished, very cautiously, and waited. The tiny screen lit up, and the words "STAND BY" appeared, to be replaced in a few seconds by "SCRIBE (FEMALE) OF THE HOUSEHOLD BAN-HARIHN, which meant he had at least dialed correctly. The screen cleared and the words were replaced by the face of his household Scribe, so distorted by distance as to be only by courtesy a face, but with the ban-harihn matrix-mark superimposed in green and yellow across the screen as security.

He spoke quickly, mindful of the com-rates at this distance.

"Scribe ban-harihn, this morning the state-of-being disk indicated some difficulty in the condition of the Khadilha Althea. Please advise if this condition could be described as an emergency."

After the usual brief lag for conversion to symbols, the reply was superimposed over the matrix-mark, and the Khadilh thought as usual that these tiny intergalactic screens became so cluttered before a conversation was terminated that one could hardly make out the messages involved.

The message in this case was "Negative," and the Khadilh smiled; the Scribe was even more mindful than he of the cost of this transmittal.

He pushed the ERASE button and finished with, "Thank you, Scribe ban-harihn. You will then prepare at once a written report, in detail, and forward it to me by the fastest available means. Should the problem intensify to emergency point, I now authorize a com-system transmittal to that effect, to be initiated by any one of my sons. Terminate."

The screen went blank and the Khadilh, just for curiosity, punched one more time the state-of-being control. The machine delivered another disk, and sure enough, there it was again, black dots, red star and all. He threw it into the disposal, shrugged his shoulders helplessly and ordered coffee. There was nothing whatever that he could do until he received the Scribe's report.

However, if it should turn out that he had wasted the cost of an intergalactic transmittal on some petty household dispute, there was going to be hell to pay, he promised himself, and a suitable punishment administered to the Khadilha by the nearest official of the Women's Discipline Unit. There certainly ought to be some way to make the state-of-being codes a bit more detailed so that everything from war to an argument with a servingwoman didn't come across on the same symbol.

The report arrived by Tele-Bounce in four days. Very wise choice, he thought approvingly, since the Bounce machinery was totally automatic and impersonal. It was somewhat difficult to read, since the Scribe had specified that it was to be delivered to him without transcription other than into verbal symbols, and it was therefore necessary for him to scan a roll of yellow paper with a message eight symbols wide and seemingly miles long. He read only enough to convince him that no problem of discretion could possibly be involved, and then he ran the thing through the transcribe slot, receiving a standard letter on white paper in return.

"To the Khadilh ban-harihn," it read, "as requested, the following report from the Scribe of his household:

Three days ago, as the Khadilh is no doubt aware, the festival of the Spring Rains was celebrated here. The entire household, with the exception of the Khadilh himself, was present at a very large and elaborate procession held to mark the opening of the Alaharibahn-khalida Trance Hours. A suitable spot for watching the procession, entirely in accordance with decorum, had been chosen by the Khadilha Althea, and the women of the household were standing in the second row along the edge of the street set aside for the women.

There had been a number of dancers, bands, and so on, followed by thirteen of the Poets of this city-cluster. The Poets had almost passed, along with the usual complement of exotic animals and mobile flowers and the like, and no untoward incident of any kind had occurred, when quite suddenly the Khadilh's daughter Jacinth was approached by (pardon my liberty of speech) the Poet Anna-Mary, who is, as the Khadilh knows, a female. The Poet leaned from her mount, indicating with her staff of bells that it was her wish to speak to the Khadilh's daughter, and halting the procession to do so. It was at this point that the incident occurred which has no doubt given rise to the variant marking in the state-of-being disk line for the Khadilha Althea. Quite unaccountably, the Khadilha, rather than sending the child forward to speak with the Poet (as would have been proper), grabbed the child Jacinth by the shoulders, whirling her around and covering her completely with her heavy robes so that she could neither speak nor see.

The Poet Anna-Mary merely bowed from her horse and signaled for the procession to continue, but she was quite white and obviously offended. The family made a show of participating in the rest of the day's observances, but the Khadilh's sons took the entire household home by mid-afternoon, thereby preventing the Khadilha from participating in the Trance Hours. This was no doubt a wise course.

What sequel there may have been to this, the Scribe does not know, as no announcement has been made to the household. The Scribe here indicates her respect and subservience to the Khadilh.

Terminate with thanks.

"Well!" said the Khadilh. He laid the letter down on the top of his desk, thinking hard, rubbing his beard with one hand.

What could reasonably be expected in the way of repercussions from a public insult to an elderly—and touchy—Poet? It was hard to say.

As the only female Poet on the planet, the Poet Anna-Mary was much alone; as her duties were not arduous, she had much time to brood. And though she was a Poet, she remained only a female, with the female's inferior reasoning powers. She was accustomed to reverent homage, to women holding up their children to touch the hem of her robe. She could hardly be expected to react with pleasure to an insult in public, and from a female.

It was at his sons that she would be most likely to strike, through the University, he decided, and he could not chance that. He had worked too hard, and they had worked too hard, to allow a vindictive female, no matter how lofty her status, to destroy what they had built up. He had better go home and leave the orchards to take care of themselves; important as the lush peaches of Earth were to the economy of his home planet, his sons were of even greater importance.

It was not every family that could boast of five sons in the University, all five selected by competitive examinations for the Major in Poetry. Sometimes a family might have two sons chosen, but the rest would be refused, as the Khadilh himself had been refused, and would then have to be satisfied with the selection of Law or Medicine or Government or some other of the Majors. He smiled proudly, remembering the respectful glances of his friends when each of his sons in turn had placed high in the examinations and had been awarded the Poet Major, his oldest son entering at the Fourth Level. And when the youngest had been chosen, thus releasing the oldest from the customary vow of celibacy—since to impose it would have meant the end of the family line, an impossible situation—the Khadilh had had difficulty in maintaining even a pretense of modesty. The meaning, of course, was that he would have as grandson the direct offspring of a Poet, something that had not happened within his memory or his father's memory. He had been given to understand, in fact, that it had been more than three hundred years

12

since all sons of any one family had entered the Poetry courses. (A family having only one son was prohibited by law from entering the Poetry Examinations, they told him.)

Yes, he must go home, and to hell with the peaches of Earth. Let them rot, if the garden-robots could not manage them.

He went to the com-system and punched through a curt transmittal of his intention, and then set to pulling the necessary strings to obtain a priority flight.

When the Khadilh arrived at his home, his sons were lined up in his study, waiting for him, each in the coarse brown student's tunic that was compulsory, but with the scarlet Poet's stripe around the hem to delight his eyes. He smiled at them, saying, "It is a pleasure to see you once more, my sons; you give rest to my eyes and joy to my heart."

Michael, the oldest, answered in kind.

"It is our pleasure to see you, Father."

"Let us all sit down," said the Khadilh, motioning them to their places about the study table that stood in the center of the room. When they were seated, he struck the table with his knuckles, in the old ritual, three times slowly.

"No doubt you know why I have chosen to abandon my orchards to the attention of the garden-robots and return home so suddenly," he said. "Unfortunately, it has taken me almost ten months to reach you. There was no more rapid way to get home to you, much as I wished for one."

"We understand, Father," said his oldest son.

"Then, Michael," went on Khadilh, "would you please bring me up to date on the developments here since the incident at the procession of the Spring Rains."

His son seemed hesitant to speak, his black brows drawn together over his eyes, and the Khadilh smiled at him encouragingly.

"Come, Michael," he said, "surely it is not courteous to make your father wait in this fashion!"

"You will realize, Father," said the young man slowly, "that it has not been possible to communicate with you since the time of your last transmittal. You will also realize that this matter has not been one about which advice could easily be requested. I have had no choice but to make decisions as best I could."

"I realize that. Of course."

"Very well, then. I hope you will not be angry, Father."

"I shall indeed be angry if I am not told at once exactly what has occurred this past ten months. You make me uneasy, my son."

Michael took a deep breath and nodded. "All right, Father," he said. "I will be brief."

"And quick."

"Yes, Father. I took our household away from the festival as soon as I decently could without creating talk; and when we arrived at home, I sent the Khadilha at once to her quarters, with orders to stay there until you should advise me to the contrary."

"Quite right," said the Khadilh. "Then what?"

"The Khadilha disobeyed me, Father."

"Disobeyed you? In what way?"

"The Khadilha Althea disregarded my orders entirely, and she took our sister into the Small Corridor, and there she allowed her to look into the cell where our aunt is kept, Father."

"My God!" shouted the Khadilh. "And you made no move to stop her?"

"Father," said Michael ban-harihn, "you must realize that no one could have anticipated the actions of the Khadilha Althea. We would certainly have stopped her had we known, but who would have thought that the Khadilha would disobey the order of an adult male? It was assumed that she would go to her quarters and remain there."

"I see."

"I did not contact the Women's Discipline Unit," Michael continued. "I preferred that such an order should come from you, Father. However, orders were given that the Khadilha should be restricted to her quarters, and no one has been allowed to see her except the servingwomen. The wires to her com-system were disconnected, and provision was made for suitable medication to be added to her diet. You will find her very docile, Father."

The Khadilh was trembling with indignation.

"Discipline will be provided at once, my son," he said.

"I apologize for the disgusting behavior of the Khadilha. But please go on—what of my daughter?"

"That is perhaps the most distressing thing of all."

"In what way?"

Michael looked thoroughly miserable.

"Answer me at once," snapped the Khadil, "and in full."

"Our sister Jacinth," said his second son, Nicolas, "was already twelve years of age at the time of the festival. When she returned from the Small Corridor, without notice to any one of us, she announced her intention by letter to the Poet Anna-Mary—her intention to compete in the examinations for the Major of Poetry."

"And the Poet Anna-Mary—"

"Turned the announcement immediately over to the authorities at the Poetry Unit," finished Michael. "Certainly she made no attempt to dissuade our sister."

"She is amply revenged then for the insult of the Khadilha," said the Khadilh bitterly. "Were there any other acts on the part of the Poet Anna-Mary?"

"None, Father. Our sister has been cloistered by government order since that time, of course, to prevent contamination of the other females."

"Oh, dear God," breathed the Khadilh, "how could such a thing have touched my household—for the second time?"

He thought a moment. "When are the examinations, then? I've lost all track of time."

"It has been ten months, Father."

"In about a month, then?"

"In three weeks."

"Will they let me see Jacinth?"

"No, Father," said Michael. "And, Father—"

"Yes, Michael?"

"It is my shame and my sorrow that this should have been the result of your leaving your household in my care."

The Khadilh reached over and grasped his hand firmly.

"You are very young, my son," he said, "and you have nothing to be ashamed of. When the females of a household take it upon themselves to upset the natural order of things and to violate the rules of decency, there is very little anyone can do."

"Thank you, Father."

"Now," said the Khadilh, turning to face them all, "I suggest that the next thing to do would be to initiate action by the Women's Discipline Unit. Do you wish me to have the Khadilha placed on Permanent Medication, my sons?"

He hoped they would not insist upon it, and was pleased to see that they did not.

"Let us wait, Father," said Michael, "until we know the outcome of the examinations."

"Surely the outcome is something about which there can be no question!"

"Could we wait, Father, all the same?"

It was the youngest of the boys. As was natural, he was still overly squeamish, still a bit tender. The Khadilh would not have had him be otherwise.

"A wise decision," he said. "In that case, once I have bathed and had my dinner, I will send for the Lawyer an-ahda. And you may go, my sons."

The boys filed out, led by the solemn Michael, leaving him with no company but the slow dance of a mobile flower from one of the tropical stars. It whirled gently in the middle of the corner hearth, humming to itself and giving off showers of silver sparks from time to time. He watched it suspiciously for a moment, and then pushed the com-system buttons for his Housekeeper. When the face appeared on the screen he snapped at it.

"Housekeeeper, are you familiar with the nature of the mobile plant that someone has put in my study?"

The Housekeeper's voice, frightened, came back at once. "The Khadilh may have the plant removed—should I call the Gardener?"

"All I wanted to know is the sex of the blasted thing," he bellowed at her. "Is it male or female?"

"Male, Khadilh, of the genus——"

He cut off the message while she was still telling him of the plant's pedigree. It was male; therefore it could stay. He would talk to it, while he ate his dinner, about the incredible behavior of his Khadilha.

The Lawyer an-ahda leaned back in the chair provided for him and smiled at his client.

"Yes, ban-harihn," he said amiably, having known the

Khadilh since they were young men at the University, "what can I do to help the sun shine more brightly through your window?"

"This is a serious matter," said the Khadilh.

"Ah."

"You heard—never mind being polite and denying it—of my wife's behavior at the procession of the Spring Rains. I see that you did."

"Very impulsive," observed the Lawyer. "Most unwise. Undisciplined."

"Indeed it was. However, worse followed."

"Oh? The Poet Anna-Mary has tried for revenge, then?"

"Not in the sense that you mean, no. But worse has happened, my old friend, far worse."

"Tell me." The Lawyer leaned forward attentively, listening, and when the Khadilh had finished, he cleared his throat.

"There isn't anything to be done, you know," he said. "You might as well know it at once."

"Nothing at all?"

"Nothing. The law provides that any woman may challenge and claim her right to compete in the Poetry Examinations, provided she is twelve years of age and a citizen of this planet. If she is not accepted, however, the penalty for having challenged and failed is solitary confinement for life, in the household of her family. And once she has announced to the Faculty by signed communication that she intends to compete, she is cloistered until the day of the examinations, and she may not change her mind. The law is very clear on this point."

"She is very young."

"She is twelve. That is all the law requires."

"It's a cruel law."

"Not at all! Can you imagine, ban-harihn, the chaos that would result if every emotional young female, bored with awaiting marriage in the women's quarters, should decide that she had a vocation and claim her right to challenge? The purpose of the law is to discourage foolish young girls from creating difficulties for their households, and for the state. Can you just imagine, if there were only a token penalty, and chaperons had to be provided by the Faculty, and separate quarters provided, and——"

"Yes, I suppose I see! But why should women be allowed to compete at all? No such idiocy is allowed in the other Professions."

"The law provides that since the Profession of Poetry is a religious office, there must be a channel provided for the rare occasion when the Creator might see fit to call a female to His service."

"What nonsense!"

"There is the Poet Anna-Mary, ban-harihn."

"And how many others?"

"She is the third."

"In nearly ten thousand years! Only three in so many centuries, and yet no exception can be made for one little twelve-year-old girl?"

"I am truly sorry, my friend," said the Lawyer. "You could try a petition to the Council, of course, but I am quite sure—*quite* sure—that it would be of no use. There is too much public reaction to a female's even attempting the examinations, because it seems blasphemous even to many very broad-minded people. The Council would not dare to make an exception."

"I could make a galactic appeal."

"You could."

"There would be quite a scandal, you know, among the peoples of the galaxy, if they knew of this penalty being enforced on a child."

"My friend, my dear ban-harihn—think of what you are saying. You would create an international incident, an intergalactic international incident, with all that implies, bring down criticism upon our heads, most surely incur an investigation of our religious customs by the intergalactic police, which would in turn call for a protest from our government, which in its turn——"

"You know I would not do it."

"I hope not. It would parallel the Trojan War for folly, my friend—all that for the sake of one female child!"

"We are a barbaric people."

The Lawyer nodded. "After ten thousand years, you know, if barbarism remains it becomes very firmly entrenched."

The Lawyer rose to go, throwing his heavy blue cloak around him. "After all," he said, "it is only one female child."

It was all very well, thought the Khadilh when his friend was gone, all very well to say that. The Lawyer no doubt never had had the opportunity to see the result of a lifetime of solitary confinement in total silence, or he would have been less willing to see a child condemned to such a fate.

The Khadilh's sister had been nearly thirty, and yet unmarried, when she had chosen to compete, and she was forty-six now. It had been an impulse of folly, born of thirty years of boredom, and the Khadilh blamed his parents. Enough dowry should have been provided to make even Grace, ugly as she was, an acceptable bride for someone, somewhere.

The room in the Small Corridor, where she had been confined since her failure, had no window, no com-system, nothing. Her food was passed through a slot in one wall, as were the few books and papers which she was allowed— all these things being very rigidly regulated by the Women's Discipline Unit.

It was the duty of the Khadilha Althea to go each morning to the narrow grate that enclosed a one-way window into the cell and to observe the prisoner inside. On the two occasions when that observation had disclosed physcial illness, a dart containing an anesthetic had been fired through the food slot, and Grace had been rendered unconscious for the amount of time necessary to let a Doctor enter the cell and attend to her. She had had sixteen years of this, and it was the Khadilha who had had to watch her, through the first years when she alternately lay stuporous for days and then screamed and begged for release for days . . . now she was quite mad. The Khadilh had observed her on two occasions when his wife had been too ill to go, and he had found it difficult to believe that the creature who crawled on all fours from one end of the room to the other, its matted hair thick with filth in spite of the servomechanisms that hurried from the walls to retrieve all waste and dirt, was his sister. It gibbered and whined and clawed at its flesh—it was hard to believe that it was human. And it had been only sixteen years. Jacinth was twelve!

The Khadilh called his wife's quarters and announced to her servingwomen that they were all to leave her. He went rapidly through the corridors of his house, over the delicate arched bridge that spanned the tea gardens around the women's quarters, and into the rooms where she stayed. He found her sitting in a small chair before her fireplace, watching the mobile plants that danced there to be near the warmth of the fire. As his sons had said, she was quite docile, and in very poor contact with reality.

He took a capsule from the pocket of his tunic and gave it to her to swallow, and when her eyes were clear of the mist of her drugged dreams, he spoke to her.

"You see that I have returned, Althea," he said. "I wish to know why my daughter has brought this ill fortune upon our household."

"It is her own idea," said the Khadilha in a bitter voice. "Since the last of her brothers was chosen, she has been thus determined, saying that it would be a great honor for our house should all of the children of ban-harihn be accepted for the faith."

It was as if a light had been turned on.

"This was not an impulse, then!" exclaimed the Khadilh.

"No. Since she was nine years old she has had this intention."

"But why was I not told? Why was I given no opportunity——" He stopped abruptly, knowing that he was being absurd. No women would bother her husband with the problems of rearing a female child. But now he began to understand.

"She did not even know," his wife was saying, "that there was a living female Poet, although she had heard from someone that such a possibility existed. It was, she insisted, a matter of knowledge of the heart. When the Poet Anna-Mary singled her out at the procession . . . why, then, she was sure. Then she knew, she said, that she had been chosen."

Of course. That in itself, being marked out for notice before the crowd, would have convinced the child that her selection was ordained by Divine choice. He could see it all now. And the Khadilha had taken the child to see her aunt in her cell in a last desperate attempt to dissuade her.

"The child is strong-willed for a female," he mused, "if the sight of poor Grace did not shake her."

His wife did not answer, and he sat there, almost too

tired to move. He was trying to place the child Jacinth in his mind's eye, but it was useless. It had been at least four years since he had seen her, dressed in a brief white shift that all little girls wore: he remembered a slender child, he remembered dark hair—but then all little girls among his people were slender and dark-haired.

"You don't even remember her," said his wife, and he jumped, irritated at her shrewdness.

"You are quite right," he said. "I don't. Is she pretty?"

"She is beautiful. Not that it matters now."

The Khadilh thought for a moment, watching his wife's stoic face, and then, choosing his words with care, he said, "It had been my intention to register a complaint with the Women's Discipline Unit for your behavior, Khadilha Althea."

"I expected you to do so."

"You have a good deal of experience with the agents of the WDU—the prospect does not upset you?"

"I am indifferent to it."

He believed her. He remembered very well the behavior of his wife at her last impregnation, for it had required four agents from the Unit to subdue her and fasten her to their marriage bed. And yet he knew that many women went willingly, even eagerly, to their appointments with their husbands. It was at times difficult for him to understand why he had not had Althea put on Permanent Medication from the very beginning; certainly, it would not have been difficult to secure permission to take a second, more womanly wife. Unfortunately he was softhearted, and she had been the mother of his eldest son, and so he had put up with her, relying upon his concubines for feminine softness and ardor. Certainly Althea had hardened with the years, not softened.

"I have decided," he finished abruptly, "that your behavior is not so scandalous as I had thought. I am not sure I would not have reacted just as you did under the circumstances, if I had known the girl's plans. I will make no complaint, therefore."

"You are indulgent."

He scanned her face, still lovely for all her years, for signs of impertinence, but there were none, and he went on: "However, you understand our eldest son must decide for himself if he wishes to forego his own complaint. Your disobedience to him wasn't your first, you know. I have become accustomed to it."

He turned on his heel and left her, amused at his own weakness, but he canceled the medication order when he went past the entrance to her quarters. She was a woman, she had meant to keep her daughter from becoming what Grace had become; it was not so hard to understand, after all.

The family did not go to the University on the day of the examinations. They waited at home, prepared for the inevitable as well as they could prepare.

Another room, near the room where Grace was kept, had been made ready by the weeping servingwomen, and it stood open now, waiting.

The Khadilh had had his wife released from her quarters for the day, since she would have only the brief moment with her daughter, and thereafter would have only the duty of observing her each morning as she did her sister-in-law. She sat at his feet now in their common room, making no sound, her face bleached white, wondering, he supposed, what she would do now. She had no other daughter; there were no other sisters. She would be alone in the household except for her servingwoman, until such a time as Michael should, perhaps, provide her with a granddaughter. His heart ached for her, alone in a household of men, and five of them, before very long, to be allowed to speak only in the rhymed couplets of the Poets.

"Father?"

The Khadilh looked up, surprised. It was his youngest son, the boy James.

"Father," said the boy, "could she pass? I mean, is it possible that she could pass?"

Michael answered for him. "James, she is only twelve, and a female. She has had no education; she can only just barely read. Don't ask foolish questions. Don't you remember the examinations?"

"I remember," said James firmly. "Still, I wondered. There is the Poet Anna-Mary."

"The third in who knows how many hundreds of years, James," Michael said. "I shouldn't count on it if I were you."

"But is it possible?" the boy insisted. "Is it possible, Father?"

"I don't think so, son," said the Khadilh gently. "It would be a very curious thing if an untrained twelve-year-old female could pass the examinations that I could not pass myself, when I was sixteen, don't you think?"

"And then," said the boy, "she may never see anyone again, as long as she lives, never speak to anyone, never look out a window, never leave that little room?"

"Never."

"That is a cruel law!" said the boy. "Why has it not been changed?"

"My son," said the Khadilh. "it is not something that happens often, and the Council has many, many other things to do. It is an ancient law, and the knowledge that it exists offers to bored young females something exciting to think about. It is intended to frighten them, my son."

"One day, when I have power enough, I shall have it changed."

The Khadilh raised his hand to hush the laughter of the older boys. "Let him alone," he snapped. "He is young, and she is his sister. Let us have a spirit of compassion in this house, if we must have tragedy."

A thought occurred to him, then. "James," he said, "you take a great deal of interest in this matter. Is it possible that you were somehow involved in this idiocy of your sister's?"

At once he knew he had struck a sensitive spot; tears sprang to the boy's eyes and he bit his lip fiercely.

"James—in what way were you involved? What do you know of this affair?"

"You will be angry, my father," said James, "but that is not the worst. What is worse is that I will have condemned my sister to——"

"James," said the Khadilh, "I have no interest in your self-accusations. Explain at once, simply and without dramatics."

"Well, we used to practice, she and I," said the boy hastily, his eyes on the floor. "I did not think I would pass, you know. I could see it—all the others would pass, and I would not, and there I would be, the only one. People would say, there he goes, the only one of the sons of the ban-harihn who could not pass the Poetry exam."

"And?"

"And so we practiced together, she and I," he said. "I would set the subject and the form and do the first stanza, and then she would write the reply."

"When did you do this? Where?"

"In the gardens, Father, ever since she was little. She's very good at it, she really is, Father."

"She can rhyme? She knows the forms?"

"Yes, Father! And she *is* good, she has a gift for it—Father, she's much better than I am. I am ashamed to say that, of a female, but it would be a lie to say anything else."

The things that went on in one's household! The Khadilh was amazed and dismayed, and he was annoyed besides. Not that it was unusual for brothers and sisters, while still young, to spend time together, but surely one of the servants, or one of the family, ought to have noticed that the two little ones were playing at Poetry?

"What else goes on in my house beneath the blind eyes and deaf ears of those I entrust with its welfare?" he demanded furiously, and no one hazarded an answer. He made a sound of disgust and went to the window to look out over the gardens that stretched down to the narrow river behind the house. It had begun to rain, a soft green rain not much more than a mist, and the river was blurred velvet through the veil of water. Another time he would have enjoyed the view; indeed, he might well have sent for his pencils and his sketching pad to record its beauty. But this was not a day for pleasure.

Unless, of course, Jacinth did pass.

It was, on the face of it, an absurdity. The examinations for Poetry were far different than those for the other Professions. In the others it was a straightforward matter: one went to the examining room, an examination was distributed, one spent perhaps six hours in such exams, and they were then scored by computer. Then, in a few days, there would come the little notice by com-system, stating that one had or had not passed the fitness exams for Law or Business or whatever.

Poetry was a different matter. There were many degrees of fitness, all the way from the First Level, which fitted a man for the lower offices of the faith, through five more subordinate levels, to the Seventh Level. Very rarely did anyone enter the Seventh Level. Since there was no question of being promoted from one level to another, a man being placed at his appropriate rank by the examinations at the very beginning, there were times when the Seventh Level remained vacant for as long as a year. Michael had been placed at the Fourth Level instead of the First, like the others of his sons, and the Khadilh had been awed at the implications.

For Poetry there was first an examination of the usual kind, marked by hand and scored by machine, just as in the other Professions. But then, if that exam was passed, there was something unique to do. The Khadilh had not passed the exam and he had no knowledge of what came next, except that it involved the computers.

"Michael," he said, musing, "how does it go exactly, the Poetry exam by the computer?"

Michael came over to stand beside him. "You mean, should Jacinth pass the written examination, even if just by chance, then what happens?"

"Yes. Tell me."

"It's simple enough. You go into the booths where the computer panels are and push a READY button. Then the computer gives you your instructions."

"For example?"

"Let's see. For example, it might say—SUBJECT: LOVE OF COUNTRY . . . FORM: SONNET. UNRESTRICTED BUT RHYMED . . . STYLE: FORMAL, SUITABLE FOR AN OFFICIAL BANQUET. And then you would begin."

"Are you allowed to use paper and pen, my son?"

"Oh, no, Father." Michael was smiling, no doubt, thought the Khadilh, at his father's innocence. "No paper or pencil. And you begin at once."

"No time to think?"

"No, Father, none."

"Then what?"

"Then, sometimes, you are sent to another computer, one that gives more difficult subjects. I suppose it must be the same all the way to the Seventh Level, except that the subject would grow more difficult."

The Khadilh thought it over. For his own office of Khadilh, which meant little more than "Administrator of Large Estates and Households," he had had to take one oral examination, and that had been in ordinary, straightforward prose, and the examiner had been a man, not a computer, and he still remembered the incredible stupidity of his answers. He had sat flabbergasted at the things that issued from his mouth, and he had been convinced that he could not possibly have passed the examination. And Jacinth was only twelve years old, with none of the training that boys received in prosody, none of the summer workshops in the different forms, scarcely even an acquaintance with the history of the classics. Surely she would be too terrified to speak? Why, the simple modesty of her femaleness ought to be enough to keep her mute, and then she would fail, even if she should somehow be lucky enough to pass the written exam. Damn the girl!

"Michael," he asked, "what is the level of the Poet Anna-Mary?"

"Second Level, Father."

"Thank you, my son. You have been very helpful—you may sit down now, if you like."

He stood a moment more, watching the rain, and then went back and sat down again by his wife. Her hands flew, busy with the little needles used to make the complicated hoods the Poets wore. She was determined that her sons should, in accordance with the ancient tradition, have every stitch of their installation garments made by her hands, although no one would have criticized her if she had had the work done by others, since she had so many sons needing the garments. He was pleased with her, for once, and he made a mental note to have a gift sent to her later.

The bells rang in the city, signaling the four o'clock Hour of Meditation, and the Khadilh's sons looked at one another, hesitating. By the rules of their Major that hour was to be spent in their rooms, but their father had specifically asked that they stay with him.

The Khadilh sighed, making another mental note, that he must sigh less. It was an unattractive habit.

"My sons," he said "you must conform to the rules of your Major. Please consider that my first wish."

They thanked him and left the room, and there he sat, watching first the darting fingers of the Khadilha and then the dancing of the mobile flowers, until shadows began to streak across the tiled floor of the room. Six o'clock came, and then seven, and still no word. When his sons returned, he sent them away crossly, seeing no reason why they should share in his misery.

By the time the double suns had set over the river he had lost the compassion he had counseled for the others and become furious with Jacinth as well as the system. That one insignificant female child could create such havoc for him and for his household amazed him. He began to understand the significance of the rule; the law began to seem less harsh. He had missed his dinner and he had spent his day in unutterable tedium. His orchards were doubtless covered with insects and dying of thirst and neglect, his bank account was depleted by the expense of the trip home, the cost of extra garden-robots on Earth, the cost of the useless visit from the Lawyer. And his nervous system was shattered, and the peace of his household destroyed. All this from the antics of one twelve-year-old female child! And when she had to be shut up, there would be the necessity of living with her mother as she watched the child deteriorate into a crawling mass of filth and madness as Grace had done. Was his family cursed, that its females should bring down the wrath of the universe at large in this manner?

He struck his fists together in rage and frustration, and the Khadilha jumped, startled.

"Shall I send for music, my husband?" she asked. "Or perhaps you would like to have your dinner served here? Perhaps you would like a good wine?"

"Perhaps a dozen dancing girls!" he shouted. "Perhaps a Venusian flame-tiger! Perhaps a parade of Earth elephants and a tentacle bird from the Extreme Moons! May all the suffering gods take pity upon me!"

"I beg your pardon," said the Khadilha. "I have angered you."

"It is not you who have angered me," he retorted; "it is that miserable female of a daughter that you bore me, who has caused me untold sorrow and expense, that has angered me!"

"Very soon now," pointed out the Khadilha softly, "she will be out of your sight and hearing forever; perhaps then she will anger you less."

The Khadilha's wit, sometimes put to uncomfortable uses, had been one of the reasons he had kept her all these years. At this moment, however, he wished her stupider and timider and a thousand light-years away.

"Must you be right, at a time like this?" he demanded. "It is unbecoming in a woman."

"Yes, my husband."

"It grows late."

"Yes, indeed."

"What could they be doing over there?"

He reached over to the com-system and instructed the Housekeeper to send someone with a videocolor console. It was just possible that somewhere in the galaxy something was happening that would distract him from his misery.

He skimmed the videobands rapidly, muttering. There was a new drama by some unknown avant-garde playwright, depicting a liaison between the daughter of a Council member and a servomechanism. There was a game of jidra, both teams apparently from the Extreme Moons, if their size could be taken as any indication. There were half a dozen variety programs, each worse than the last. Finally he found a newsband and leaned forward, his ear caught by the words of the improbably sleek young man reading the announcements.

Had he said—yes! He had. He was announcing the results of the examinations in Poetry. "—ended at four o'clock this afternoon, with only eighty-three candidates accepted out of almost three thousand who—"

"Of course!" he shouted. How stupid he had been not to have realized, sooner, that since all members of Poetry were bound by oath to observe the four o'clock Hour of Meditation, the examinations would have had to end by four o'clock! But why, then, had no one come to notify them or to return their daughter? It was very near nine o'clock.

The smallest whisper of hope touched him. It was possible, just possible, that the delay was because even the callous members of the Poetry Unit were finding it difficult to condemn a little girl to a life of solitary confinement. Perhaps they were meeting to discuss it, perhaps something was being arranged, some loophole in the law being found that could be used to prevent such a travesty of justice.

He switched off the video and punched the call numbers of the Poetry Unit on the com-system. At once the screen was filled by the embroidered hood and bearded face of a

Poet, First Level, smiling helpfully through the superimposed matrix-mark of his household.

The Khadilh explained his problem, and the Poet smiled and nodded.

"Messengers are on their way to your household at this moment, Khadilh ban-harihn," he said. "We regret the delay, but it takes time, you know. All these things take time."

"What things?" demanded the Khadilh. "And why are you speaking to me in prose? Are you not a Poet?"

"The Khadilh seems upset," said the Poet in a soothing voice. "He should know that those Poets who serve the Poetry Unit as communicators are excused from the laws of verse-speaking while on duty."

"Someone is coming now?"

"Messengers are on their way."

"On foot? By Earth-style robot-mule? Why not a message by com-system?"

The Poet shook his head. "We are a very old profession, Khadilh ban-harihn. There are many traditions to be observed. Speed, I fear, is not among those traditions."

"What message are they bringing?"

"I am not at liberty to tell you that," said the Poet patiently.

Such control! thought the Khadilh. Such unending saintlike tolerance! It was maddening.

"Terminate with thanks," said the Khadilh, and turned off the bland face of the Poet. At his feet the Khadilha had set aside her work and sat trembling. He reached over and patted her hand, wishing there were some comfort he could offer.

Had they better go ahead and call for dinner? He wondered if either of them would be able to eat.

"Althea," he began, and at that moment the serving-woman showed in the messengers of the Poetry Unit, and the Khadilh rose to his feet.

"Well?" he demanded abruptly. He would be damned if he was going to engage in the usual interminable preliminaries. "Where is my daughter?"

"We have brought your daughter with us, Khadilh ban-harihn."

"Well, where is she?"

"If the Khadilh will only calm himself."

"I am calm! Now where is my daughter?"

The senior messenger raised one hand, formally, for silence, and in an irritating singsong he began to speak.

"The daughter of the Khadilh ban-harihn will be permitted to approach and to speak to her parents for one minute only, by the clock which I hold, giving to her parents whatever message of farewell she should choose. Once she has given her message, the daughter of the Khadilh will be taken away and it will not be possible for the Khadilh or his household to communicate with her again except by special petition from the Council."

The Khadilh was dumbfounded. He could feel his wife shaking uncontrollably beside him—was she about to cause a second scandal?

"Leave the room if you cannot control your emotion, Khadilha," he ordered her softly, and she responded with an immediate and icy calm of bearing. Much better.

"What do you mean," he asked the messenger, "by stating that you are about to take my daughter away again? Surely it is not the desire of the Council that she be punished outside the confines of my house!"

"Punished?" asked the messenger. "There is no punishment in question, Khadilh. It is merely that the course of study which she must follow henceforth cannot be provided for her except at the Temple of the University."

It was the Khadilh's turn to tremble now. She had passed!

"Please," he said hoarsely, "would you make yourself clear? Am I to understand that my daughter has passed the examination?"

"Certainly," said the messenger. "This is indeed a day of great honor for the household of the ban-harihn. You can be most proud, Khadilh, for your daughter has only just completed the final examination and has been placed in Seventh Level. A festival will be declared, and an official announcement will be made. A day of holiday will be ordered for all citizens of the planet Abba, in all city-clusters and throughout the countryside. It is a time of great rejoicing!"

The man went on and on, his curiously contrived-sounding remarks unwinding amid punctuating sighs and nods from the other messengers, but the Khadilh did not hear any more. He sank back in his chair, deaf to the list of the multitude of honors and happenings that would come to pass as a result of this extraordinary thing. Seventh Level! How could such a thing be?

Dimly he was aware that the Khadilha was weeping quite openly, and he used one numb hand to draw her veils across her face.

"Only one minute, by the clock," the messenger was saying. "You do understand? You are not to touch the Poet-Candidate, nor are you to interfere with her in any way. She is allowed one message of farewell, nothing more."

And then they let his daughter, this stranger who had performed a miracle, whom he would not even have recognized in a crowd, come forward into the room and approach him. She looked very young and tired, and he held his breath to hear what she would say to him.

However, it was no message of farewell that she had to give them. Said the Poet-Candidate, Seventh Level, Jacinth ban-harihn: "You will send someone at once to inform my Aunt Grace that I have been appointed to the Seventh Level of the Profession of Poetry; permission has been granted by the Council for the breaking of her solitary confinement for so long as it may take to make my aunt understand just what has happened."

And then she was gone, followed by the messengers, leaving only the muted, tinkling showers of sparks from the dancing flowers and the soft drumming of the rain on the roof to punctuate the silence.

Interlude

THE ROLL OF IAMBS AND THE CLANG OF SPONDEES

"Father?"

"Yes, my son?" The eminent Doctor ban-Claryk spoke abstractedly, his mind not at all on the boy who sat at his side. He was watching the threedy projection that filled the corner of the room, spreading across the white wall of the living semblance of the hills outside the capital city of Abba. Alsabaid, the Jewel City, lay in the arm of the deep green river, and about it curved the even greener mountains, little more than hills now with their advanced age. The threedy moved in now, outlining less sharply the panorama of summer day and sky, centering on the narrow gray bridge that spanned one loop of the river. The battle bridge.

"Father?" the boy said again, and ban-Claryk turned to face him, sorry for his discourtesy. To be discourteous to a child was only to ensure his future discourtesy to others.

"I'm sorry, Nilder," he said, "my mind was not here but out there, on that bridge. What is it?"

"Well," said the boy, "it seems to me that nothing's happening. How can it be a war—and nothing be happening?"

Doctor ban-Claryk shook his head at his son, smiling, but he spoke sternly.

"A war is not intended to be an entertainment for children," he said. "I told you, don't you remember, that there will be very little to see."

"But in my books, Father——"

"In your books, my son, you read of the ridiculous excesses of primitive civilizations! This is the thirty-first century, not the Dark Ages. It has been many thousands of years since any violence was allowed among our people, any sort of *spectacle* of battle."

The boy drew a sharp breath and leaned forward, staring in disbelief at the projection where figures were now moving in solemn procession onto the narrow bridge.

"Father!" he said, his voice thin with shock. "Father, that is a female at the head of the column!"

"It is indeed, Nilder."

"But how can a female fight in a war? Only the Poets are allowed to do battle!"

"And the Servicemen, who bear the pain."

"But the actual battle—that is for the Poets, Father!"

Doctor ban-Claryk nodded sadly.

"Yes, my son," he said. "Precisely. And that is exactly what the war is about, you see."

On the bridge, alone in the whipping wind from the river, the Poet Jacinth ban-harihn stood in a battle robe of rough scarlet linen and waited for the challenger, her heart sick and heavy, her sorrow too deep even for tears. She had wept all the night before; now her eyes were dry and she felt her whole being dry too, a husk standing there for the wind to rattle.

At the crest of a low hill she saw a figure marching along at the head of an army identical in number and in dress to the one that stood in ranks on the banks of the river behind her. The battle bridge apparently noted his appearance as well, for the War Computer rose at once from the center of the bridge and stood, stolid and square, a barrier between the two Poets.

The Poet Avhador approached rapidly, took the bridge in three strides, and faced Jacinth across the War Computer's black back.

"Greetings, Poet Jacinth, on this day
  When you shall see your title torn away!"

said Avhador, inclining his head the ritual quarter of an inch due a female of high birth, but not the deep bow due a Poet.

Jacinth gathered her mind carefully, placing the rule of tranquillity upon herself without haste, her face blank of any reaction to his rudeness. She was determined not to allow his deliberate provocations to upset her in any way. The one hundred men who stood now at attention on the riverbank, five lines of twenty in black robes of war, wearing the ritual battle masks, were totally dependent upon her clearness of mind.

She smiled, when she was ready, and bowed deeply, the full ritual obeisance to a Poet, but she made no answer.

The War Computer waited, humming to itself, all its little buttons blinking their readiness. It was very sleek, and very black, and deadly in its efficiency. Jacinth loathed the sight of it.

"Father?"

"Yes?"

"What is going to happen now? What are they going to do?"

The Doctor shrugged. "It's quite simple. They are going to compose sixteen lines of poetry, in four sets of four lines—four quatrains. The pattern of rhyme must be abba, the subject must be the subject of the war. Since the Poet Avhador is the challenger he must give the first line. The Poet Jacinth will give the second, and Avhador must then give the third, which must rhyme with hers. The Poet Jacinth must then finish the quatrain with a fourth line, which must rhyme with the first one given by Avhador. The order then changes, with the Poet Jacinth giving the first line of the second quatrain."

"That's all?" the boy demanded.

"Yes. It's not difficult. It's the sort of form you do in school."

The boy considered for a moment.

"They should do something harder than that," he said scornfully, "if they're going to call it a war! That's only baby Poetry—I could do that!"

"Ah, but there's a difference," said his father.

"And what is that?"

"When small children compose a line of Poetry, no one else has to suffer if the line is not a good one."

"Oh. Oh, I see."

The boy was quiet for a moment, watching, and then he asked, "Father? What are they doing now?"

"Praying. I hope."

The Poet Jacinth was very much aware of her responsibility to the men who were her army. She shivered in the wind, damp and chill even now in early summer, and waited for the challenge.

Avhador raised his hands above his head. He was ready.

She held her breath; if she missed a word it would not be repeated.

"NO FEMALE MAY STAND IN THE PLACE OF A MAN!" Avhador flung at her, and dropped his arms to his sides.

She weighed the line rapidly, noting the trochaic meter, the subtle internal rhyme, the fact that he had challenged by stating the thesis of the war.

"YET THE LIGHT CAN CHOOSE ONLY THE RIGHT," she replied.

"AND A TAMPERING BROTHER MAY TRAVEL BY NIGHT!" hissed Avhador, not pausing even for a second.

Jacinth recoiled, her indrawn breath hissing through her teeth. The other was mad, to accuse her brothers of having tampered with the computers in the examinations that had named her a Poet! If he were to win the war he would be very fortunate indeed if he did not have to do battle again for the insult to her family.

"AND A FOOL MAKES THE NOISES HE CAN," she said with contempt, the line dropping from her tongue almost unconsciously.

And then she turned pale. She might well have sacrificed this quatrain for the sake of a flippant insult, badly stated, empty of internal rhyme. What *had* it had to recommend it? A minor hissing assonance, perhaps. She would have to be more careful, much more careful, of her temper.

The Poet Avhador ignored her, standing rigid and staring fixedly ahead. To be called a fool by a female, before all the watching citizenry of the planet, was very probably a possibility that had never occurred to him. And since he was bound by the rules of war he could neither insult her in return, nor call for a Women's Discipline Unit, nor even formally chastise her. The frustration of it showed in his face, which was alternately white with rage and flushed with humiliation.

The War Computer was making satisfied noises, humming and chuckling to itself, rapidly reviewing the four lines of the first quatrain.

"Now, Father, now what happens? What happens next?"

"Now comes the price of war," said ban-Claryk. "The Computer will judge the lines of the quatrain by rhyming pairs, and of each pair it will choose that line which is superior. And then the pain centers will be activated."

"Father—is it a terrible pain?"

"It is direct stimulation of the pain centers of the brain, my son. There is no more dreadful agony known—and those men must stay on their feet as long as they are still alive."

"Some die, Father?"

"Some. The weaker ones."

"And the Poets feel no pain?"

"No, of course not."

"But that's not fair, Father!"

"My son," chided the man, "you are thinking like a woman. The lives of the armies depend upon the clarity of the Poets' minds, and the Poets can do battle only if they are at the peak of their attention. How could they function if they bore the pain of the War Computers? How could they compose? And you must realize, Nilder, what an unspeakable punishment it must be to hear the screams of agony from one hundred men standing behind you who have counted on you to see that they were spared that agony."

As he spoke a small panel on the front of the War Computer lit up, and the screams rose, screams more like the howling of maddened animals than the cries of men. The howling seemed to last forever, although each administration of pain was limited to forty seconds, with a respite of twenty seconds before the next one. What, ban-Claryk wondered, must it be like during that respite, knowing that the second dose of punishment was almost upon you? He shuddered.

"Father?"

"Yes?"

"I don't want to see any more, Father."

"But you must," said ban-Claryk grimly. "You must see what war is like—perhaps then when you are grown you will not be a party to such folly."

"But why are they doing it, Father? How can they do such things?"

"Well," said the man, biting off the words as if they tasted foul to him, "although the Holy Light Itself chose to make of the female Jacinth a Poet of the Seventh Level, our Poet Avhador has taken it upon himself to deny the Light that privilege. He has declared himself in a holy war, declared himself a purifier of Poetry, claiming that it is his duty to purge the holy profession of this female . . . and as you can see, my son, he is being roundly punished for his blasphemy. It was his men who took both rounds of the Pain for the first quatrain."

The army of the Poet Avhador had at last ceased to scream, and the lighted panel of the War Computer had gone dark again. Jacinth fought a rising gorge. She could not afford the luxury of sickness; she was more determined than ever that no round of that agony was to touch her men, and yet sick that by sparing her own troops she must inflict it upon the others.

Her hatred for Avhador so suffused her that she felt she must be ablaze with it . . . she fought to master herself, lest she speak too quickly. It was by passion and hasty action that wars were lost, and that men died, as two men of the army of Avhador lay dead now, their agony-twisted faces hidden behind the ritual war masks.

She raised her hands high, waited a courteous second to be sure of her opponent's attention, and threw the first line of the second quatrain at him with what she hoped was calm precision. She must be a dart of light, a spear of fire, a laser's cobweb tongue; this was no place for clubs and cudgels and the swung mace.

"LET HIM WHO WOULD QUESTION THE LIGHT BEAR THE SMITING!"

"LET HER WHO DEBASES THE LIGHT BEAR THE SHAME!"

"LET HIM WHO CRIES LIES BEAR THE PAIN OF THE FLAME!"

"FOR A BLASPHEMOUS WRONG THERE IS ONLY ONE RIGHTING!"

"That was a bad line, Father!" cried the boy, watching the rows of tiny lights flickering on the War Computer. "He's lost again, he's lost again!"

"If even you can recognize that, my son," said his father sadly, "then he is lost indeed. Nonetheless, a boy of nine does not refer to a Poet of the Sixth Level as 'he.' "

"I beg your pardon, Father."

There was a silence, and then the boy said, "That can't be right!"

"What can't be right?"

"One round went to the Poet Jacinth, and the other to the Poet Avhador! How could that be?"

"Well . . . that is difficult for me to say. I am a Doctor and the rules of Poetry are not my strongest suit. However, I would venture to say that the War Computer felt that the Poet Jacinth gave a poor challenge in her first line. Do you remember it, Nilder?"

"Yes . . . 'Let him who would question the Light bear the smiting.' "

"That's it. Now consider it. What an ugly sound it has . . . it's very bad, Nilder. Very hard to say, and unpleasant to the ear."

"Perhaps that was the reason, then, Father."

"I think so, yes. But later, when it's all over, there will be an analysis on the com-system, and we can see what the War Computer actually did."

"Oh, I didn't know that! That's good."

Jacinth had known at once how bad the line was. Despite her mental self-admonishment, she had flung that first line in passion and hatred, and it had been worthless. For that moment's indulgence of her own emotions, she had lost one of her men and who knew how many others had had their minds destroyed forever! No one bore much of the pain administered by the War Computer without permanent damage, and it was for that reason that no man might be required to serve twice in the armies of Abba.

She knew, too, and it was a bitter knowledge, that had she not been a woman the Council would never have permitted a war for such a petty cause. There were those in the Council yet, after all these years, who would have rejoiced to see Avhador win and herself exposed as a fraud, curse them for the blackness of their souls!

It was Avhador's turn to challenge. The score stood now at three to one. She intended to hold the pain rounds her men bore to that figure, and might the Light forgive her that even one had gone past her guard. She held herself in readiness, and the Poet Avhador raised his hands.

"Is it over, Father? Is that the end?"

"Yes, my son. The Light be praised, it is over."

"And the Poet Jacinth has won the war! A female!"

The Doctor did not answer. He went to his com-set and pushed the stud that would inactivate the threedy projection.

"Father?"

"Yes, Nilder?"

"What will the Poet Avhador do now? His men took seven of the eight rounds, and eleven died, because he could not even do battle with a *female!* What will he do now?"

The Doctor made a sound of utter contempt.

"If he has any worth at all," he said, "he will request a ritual death of the Doctors. And that speedily."

"Perhaps it will be you who sends him into the Light, Father!"

"I, kill a Poet? Let us hope, my son, that it will not be my misfortune to be chosen for so repugnant a duty."

"I am sorry, Father."

"And let us also hope . . ."

"Yes, Father?"

"And let us also hope that there will be no more of this folly of war and battle and pain upon our world. See to it that you grow to be a man who knows that the job of a man is to give life and to maintain it, and to cherish it, not to destroy it."

"Yes, my father."

"And now we will watch the analysis by the War Computer. You will please be very attentive."

"Yes, my father."

And then the boy sighed happily.

"That was quite a war!" he said.

ABBA

Chapter 1

She stood before him, the skin that was normally the color of coffee with lots of cream flushed almost rose with her anger, and stamped her foot.

"I know what will happen!" she said, spitting the words at him. "You will say you are going away for just a little while, but you will be gone for ever and ever."

"It's only because you are so young, Ratha, that it seems that way," Coyote said patiently. "Even if this assignment took longer than any of us expect, even at the very worst it couldn't keep me away more than three months."

"How many days is that?"

"Ninety. Almost a hundred."

"If I cry for a hundred days," she said, raising both hands in front of her face, spreading her fingers wide and peering at him through them, "I will be ugly before you come back. No one will ever want to look at me again, and it will be your fault."

"Oh, Ratha," Coyote sighed, "what am I going to do with you?"

How many times, since she was born, had he asked himself that question?

"If you keep on like this," he said carefully, "you will have to be punished."

"Ha!" She tossed her head at him, flipping the long silky mane of red-brown hair. "You can't do it—you never can!"

Coyote stared at her, angry now himself, and she stared back, not giving an inch. He felt ridiculous. Here he was, the most powerful mass projective telepath in Three Galaxies, able to control huge crowds at distances of miles, and he could not manage one small, furious five-year-old girl.

He turned to the woman who sat beside him and asked, "Do you suppose her mother could have managed her?"

Tzana Kai smiled at him, a very sarcastic smile. "I'm quite sure she could have," said Tzana, "and so could you, if you had any guts at all."

"I won't stay with you, Tzana," said the child. "I already said I won't."

"Go, then," said Tzana crisply. "That might be the best thing of all, since your father is a total eunuch where you're concerned."

"What's a eunuch?"

"No balls, my dear."

"Are there such things?"

"There used to be, long ago."

Ratha shook her head in amazement. "What use would they be?" she demanded.

"Tzana" Coyote began, but she hushed him immediately.

"Wait," she said.

"Why?"

"Well, look at her!"

"So?"

"She's thinking it over. Now—here it comes."

"If you are saying that I can go," said the child carefully, "but you were on Coyote's side before, then you are playing a trick on me."

"Not at all," said Tzana. "In fact, it was you who convinced me that you should go."

"How?" asked Ratha and Coyote together.

"When you said that your father was never able to punish you. I realized then that it would be very simple for him to punish you on Abba, because he won't have to do it himself."

Coyote opened his mouth and Tzana kicked him brutally on the ankle and he closed it again.

"Why?" asked Ratha. "Explain, please."

"On the planet Abba they have a very useful thing,"

44

said Tzana, "called the 'Women's Discipline Unit.' Any man who is having any sort of difficulty with a female of his household doesn't have to do any punishing. In fact, it would be beneath him to do so. He just goes to his com-set, punches out a call to the Women's Discipline Unit, and one of their men comes and gets the woman and takes her away and does the punishing for him."

"I would never——" began Coyote, and Tzana kicked him again.

"Wait!" she said.

Ratha clasped her hands behind her back and glared at the floor, thinking the whole thing through.

"It's a very good thing," observed Tzana softly, "that she's not psi-kinetic."

"Why?"

"Because she would keep making holes in the floor."

Ratha looked up at them.

"All right," she said, "I will stay with Tzana."

"Good," said Tzana Kai. "That's very sensible."

"But see here," protested Coyote, "I don't want her to agree to do something because of fear! I don't care to be obeyed because she's afraid of me."

Ratha's clear laugh cut across his words and Tzana nodded grimly.

"Don't be ridiculous," she said. "That child is not afraid of anything in this universe."

"Then why did she give in?"

"Because," said Tzana patiently, "she now believes what you told her before. That if you were accompanied by a female, even a very small female, your whole life would be impossibly complicated and the assignment would take twice as long. That's all."

Coyote sighed. "She couldn't have just taken my word for it?"

"I thought," said Ratha solemnly, "that you were making it worse than it really was."

"Exaggerating?"

"Yes."

"And now you don't any more?"

The child shook her head. "Not any more," she said. "Tzana doesn't do that."

"But I do?"

"Yes, you do. You do it all the time."

45

Coyote gritted his teeth, and Tzana grinned at him.

"You see what an insufferable little beast you've made of her?" she said. "Good thing you're going; perhaps I can teach her some manners while you're gone."

"Now, Tzana," Coyote said hastily, "I don't want you doing anything——"

And then he stopped. Far from being intimidated by Tzana, Ratha stood, hands on her hips, laughing at the two of them. He threw up his hands in despair.

"I give up!" he said. "I don't understand any of this."

Tzana reached over and touched his cheek. "Just go on to Abba, love, and take care of whatever it is that needs taking care of. Ratha and I will manage, won't we, Ratha?"

"We always do, you know," said the child. "We just always do."

Even the Fish was appalled by Abba, and he didn't appall easy. He had explained the assignment to Coyote with a faint air of distaste, like a Martian Orthodox Flannist discussing poultry farming.

"The whole system is ridiculous," Coyote told him. "How can such a thing be allowed to go on?"

The Fish shrugged. "It's a vast improvement over what they had before," he said.

"That's a matter of opinion."

"Let me review the basic facts for you," said the Fish. "And don't, for the Light's sake, go tramping about Abba suggesting improvements in their social system. In the first place it's none of our business. In the second place, they have ten thousand years of *recorded* history, and evidence of thirty thousand before that, and they look upon the rest of us as kindergarteners at the business of being civilizations."

"Which effectively disproves the idea that the progress of a culture through time is necessarily a progress from worse to better."

"Quite so," said the Fish. "But you must admit that what they've done shows a high degree of practical expertise at social manipulation."

"I've forgotten the details."

The Fish rubbed his hands together and smiled. He was always pleased when Coyote had to listen to him.

"I could just go check out a microfilm on it," said Coyote at once, noting the pleasure.

The Fish raised his hand.

"That won't be necessary," he said smoothly. "I have it all on the tip of my tongue."

Coyote said nothing.

"When our space colonists worked their way out to the middle of the Second Galaxy," the old man went on, "they found Abba already settled, as I said before. The people were humanoid, indistinguishable from Earth-type humans except for the presence of three extra ribs and some sort of difference in the liver that escapes me."

"Not important," said Coyote.

"At that time the Galactic Council was already well established, the Federation was a firm entity, and there were many very obvious advantages to Federation membership. It was almost unknown for a planet to refuse membership—however, in this case the Federation wasn't offering."

He pressed a stud on his desk and a threedy flashed on the wall behind him. Coyote stared at it and shuddered.

"Exactly," said the Fish. "The colonists reacted as you did, with total repulsion. They found a civilization at a high degree of technological advancement, the male citizens living in luxury, and all the females in breeding pens, with stables for inclement weather, treated *precisely* as we treat domestic animals."

"Sick," said Coyote. "Just plain sick."

"It seemed perfectly reasonable to the Abbans," the Fish went on, "that being the way they had always done things, and so far as they knew the only way there *was* to do things. But it was most definitely not acceptable to the members of the Galactic Federation. The impasse was solved by a gentleman named David Rutherford Williams, who went out to Abba with a proposal and managed to produce the ingenious compromise they have today."

"The harem. The Women's Discipline Unit."

"Well, I agree with you that it doesn't seem very enlightened, Mr. Jones, but it was at least a form of society that was tolerable to the members of the Federation at the time. And you must admit that it shows a high degree of organization for a society so totally un-Earth-like to be able to superimpose a sort of amalgamation of ancient Egypt, Arabia, and the French diplomatic service over its own culture. Practically overnight."

"How long did it take?"

"Less than six months, as I recall. Williams showed them a stack of threedies, they went 'Ah, yes' at him, their carpenters and masons trotted off and built women's quarters to specifications, and it all worked. Amazing."

"Does it really work?"

The Fish shrugged again. "Who can tell? It seems to. At least, since the Abban conversion to the religion of the Holy Light, they believe that women have souls."

Coyote made a sound of disgust, and the Fish raised a warning hand.

"I think you'll be surprised," he said. "I really do, Mr. Jones. If you expect primitive barbarians lurching about whipping their concubines you are going to be very surprised. Why don't you wait and see? And since no interference is allowed in any case, you might just as well relax."

"Oh, all right," said Coyote. "I'll try not to be so damned provincial. For the moment. Now let me see if I have the details of this assignment straight."

"Good."

"The Abbans have a lady whose profession is Poetry— is that right? It sounds odd."

"No, that's right. The Professions on Abba are like religions elsewhere. One joins for life, wears a special costume, and so on. Women are admitted only to Poetry. Poetry is a religious office, even in *their* culture, and someone managed to convince them that it was possible that a female might have a religious vocation."

"Okay. Now this lady is of very high status."

"Poet of the Seventh Level. There is no higher status on Abba."

"How the hell can that be? If women are barely tolerated——"

"Wait and see."

"All right—but I don't like it. Now, this woman is being poisoned."

"Correct."

"And because of her status, her death would be a planet-wide scandal."

"Correct again."

"And you're sending out a member of the Tri-Galactic Intelligence Service, a TGIS agent, to catch a bloody *poisoner?*"

"Abba pays very heavy taxes to the Federation, Mr. Jones," said the Fish. "They are an influential planet, with great power. They inform us that the taboo structure on Abba makes it impossible to deal with the situation as they would if the victim of the poisoning were not both female and a Poet, and they have asked us—politely—for an agent to help. We are glad to oblige."

"We are, eh?"

"We are. And you should be delighted, Mr. Jones. For once you have an assignment that a child could handle. No danger. No messy counter-espionage. Just an ordinary garden-variety poisoner. You will have luxurious quarters, your every wish granted, and you should be back here in about ten weeks, give or take a week or two. Why are you bitching? Perhaps you cannot bear to be separated from your charming Tzana Kai even so briefly?"

Coyote snorted into his beard, and the Fish smiled.

"Is it an ego problem then, Mr. Jones?" he cooed. "Perhaps you feel that an agent of your stature should not have to stoop to dealing with such a minute problem?"

That was it, of course. Coyote rather fancied himself beyond routine bogeyman-chasing assignments. But he wasn't about to answer. He shut his mouth tight and let the Fish giggle.

"Look on it as a kind of vacation," said the old man. "Like a summer by the sea, all expenses paid."

Coyote left as abruptly as he could, leaving the Fish snickering at his deck. He could have turned the assignment down, of course; since it was not a matter of intergalactic security he was not obligated to take it.

But he had a reason. He had never, not once in his entire life, seen a subjugated woman.

Curiosity took Coyote lots of places.

Chapter 2

Coyote arrived at the rocketport of Abba's capitol city at dawn, an arrangement not wholly to his liking. Cities tended to be gray and ghastly and deserted in the early morning hours; he had dismal memories of at least half a dozen where he had waited, too awake to sleep, for the city to wake up with him and begin its day.

He stepped off the rocket into an embarking-tube, and stood restlessly while its moving belt carried him into the station. He had only two fellow-travelers, a pair of Abbans in dark blue robes with a broad stripe of purple at hem and wrist. He looked at the chart in his tourist's manual, running his finger down the list. There it was: Dark blue robe, purple stripe—Profession, Law. That meant that they were lawyers, or judges, or politicians, or diplomats, or possibly policemen, all these being subsumed under the single heading, Law. They rode quietly behind him, murmuring in soft, well-bred voices, and he smiled. No whips yet. No litters carried by concubines.

At the end of the embarking-tube there were two waiting gentlemen, in robes vertically striped in light blue and tan, alternating. He checked the list quickly. Profession—Service. That could mean almost anything. Whatever it meant, they were apparently here to serve *him*. One stepped forward and took his kit, the other murmured, "Citizen Jones? We are honored; this way, please," and they went off with him in tow. Just as the Fish had promised him. Lots of service.

He had no time to catch more than a jumbled, hasty impression of the enormous rocketport before he was outside again, half out of breath, and then to his amazement he stood before a light four-wheeled vehicle, pulled by a pair of—what? He didn't have any idea.

"What is it? Are they?" he asked bluntly. "The animals, I mean?"

"They are *thaans*," said one of the gentlemen, flawless Panglish dropping from his lips like sweet oil flowing. "A fine animal, Citizen Jones. Almost like the ancient Earth animal that was called a mule, but rather more elegant. Won't you get in, Citizen?"

A mule? Even an elegant mule! To come here by government rocket, in hibernation, and then board a mule-drawn carriage? Coyote chuckled.

"You are amused, Citizen?" asked one of the men. "Perhaps you would share your joke with us?"

He told them and they smiled.

"We have whatever you might require in the way of transport," said the one who had asked him why he laughed. "Personal fliers, ground-cars, moving belts, hover-buses, whatever you prefer. But this is your first visit to our city, Citizen, and you will see it far better by thaan-carriage, if you will allow us to show you."

"Oh, certainly, certainly!" Coyote agreed hastily, afraid that he had been rude already. It always happened, but usually he managed to get through the first half hour on a planet without putting his foot in his mouth. This might well turn to be a new record. He stepped into the carriage, hoping he looked eager, and sat down. The two men followed him, one took the reins, both smiled reassuringly, and they were off.

"My name is ban-Ness," said the driver. "Joel ban-Ness. It will require most of my attention to take us to our destination, and so my assistant will tell you of our city as we go along. He is of the household of Halfa, and is called Nikolas. Nikolas ban-Halfa. You may trust him implicitly; he is one of the most able guides in all of the capitol."

Nikolas ban-Halfa took up the conversation without so much as a pause. "Look around you, my friend," he said. "Look around you and know that I envy you. To come for the first time to Alsabaid is indeed a happiness to be treasured. This, Citizen Jones, is Alsabaid, the jewel of Abba."

The name "Alsabaid" meant just that, Coyote knew from the tourist manual. "Sabaid" was Abban for "jewel," and the place was well named. Coyote stared at it, half-hearing the guide's steady murmur of information beside him. The city glowed in the morning light, every street running under a deep green arch of ancient trees that met and mingled their leaves above the men's heads. The buildings were white, and of a curious shape, square at the bottom but with tapering walls; some were topped with pointed domes; about all of them ran balconies and verandahs of metal lace. Down from the balconies poured flowering vines, scarlet and amber and pale yellow, deep purple and brilliant blue. The morning sun stained the white walls in yellow and rose. At every intersection Coyote caught glimpses of the beauty the arching trees hid from him. Graceful bridges, flights of red-brick steps that wound up low hills, great buildings that must have been temples or cathedrals, small parks filled with fountains and flowers. The people were already up and moving in the streets, even at this hour, and they formed a patchwork in the colored robes that marked the Professions, blending and changing, sounding the same ten notes, a mobile tapestry for the pleasure of the eye.

Ban-Halfa's lecture went on without a break, and Coyote let it flow and gawked shamelessly about him like the most rank of tourists. He had never seen a city like this before, nor was he likely to do so again. No one had time these days to put loving thought and care into the building of cities, except to be sure that their power plants and sewage systems worked properly, that the recycling mains were adequate, and that the connections to the central computers were correctly set up. Alsabaid was an ancient city, a city laid out thousands and thousands of years ago by men who had the time and the inclination to do it properly. He would have to take some threedies home to Ratha, especially now since she admitted to suspecting him of chronic exaggeration.

"Citizen Jones?"

"Yes?" he said quickly, hoping he had missed nothing of importance. "I'm sorry I'm a little stunned by your jewel city."

"I understand," said ban-Ness. "I wanted you to know that we are taking you to breakfast at the Palace of Law. His Excellency, Chief of Legislators, Ruler of all Abba, awaits you there."

"At this hour?" Coyote was amazed.

"Oh, certainly," said the Abban. "No man of Abba would lie in bed after the sun has risen, and waste the best portion of the day."

"But surely," said Coyote, "I don't really need to see the Chief of Legislators himself. Wouldn't just one of your heads of police be sufficient?"

"No, no," said ban-Ness firmly. "This is a matter of the very gravest importance to all of us. The Chief of Legislators holds the safety and happiness of the Poet Jacinth as dear as does any one of us. He would not think of turning over to some lesser person the task of informing you of our difficulty."

"I am honored," said Coyote at once. This, he had been told, was the all-purpose phrase of Abba. In any emergency one need only decide between "I am honored" and "I am ashamed" and everything else would take care of itself.

The carriage was nearing the heart of the city now, and he saw the Palace of Law ahead of them, recognizing it from the tourist threedies he had hurried through at Mars-Central before leaving. It was surrounded by gardens, and every one of them was choked with young men in the brown tunics of students, every tunic bordered with the dark blue and purple stripes that marked them as Majors in Law. They seemed happy; he wondered if their wives were. Or their concubines, or whatever they had.

"May students marry?" he asked suddenly, pointing at a group of tunic-clad young men.

"Not usually, no," said ban-Halfa, as the other man drew the carriage up to the front of the Palace of Law. "When they have finished their training in their Major, then their fathers arrange marriages for them, but not generally before. It would be very foolish to do otherwise; they have no time for females."

They stepped out of the carriage and the thaans' reins were taken by another man in the tan-and-blue robes. Coyote followed the others up the marble steps, down a corridor, and through an arched door into a huge room with walls of dark blue, bordered in intricate patterns of deep purple tile. At the far end of the room windows taller than he was looked out over the gardens and the streets. The room was empty, but as they entered, another member of the Profession of Service came forward to greet them from a niche in the far wall.

"Citizen Jones," he murmured. "Citizen ban-Ness. Citizen ban-Halfa. You are welcome here. Citizen Jones, our city is your city."

There was a rapid flow of phrases in Abban, and then the greeter—Coyote assumed that must be his function—stepped to the niche in the wall from which he had come and struck a silver bell with a hammer of the same metal.

"You may go on in now," he said then, bowing slightly. "His Excellency is expecting you."

Coyote followed the two Abbans to the door, and then, to his surprise, they fell back and motioned to him that he was to go on. What were they called, he wondered—servants? Servitors? And then he remembered. The list in the handbook had told him; they were called Servicemen. Apparently an agent of TGIS might eat with His Excellency, Chief of Legislators, but a Serviceman might not. He went with what he hoped was a confident step into the smaller room, and held out his hands to clasp those of the tall, white-haired man who waited for him there. He too wore a dark blue robe; the purple stripes were perhaps a bit wider, the fabric perhaps a bit more luxurious, otherwise there was no indication that this was the chief official of an entire planet.

"Your Excellency," said Coyote, and then added for good measure, "I am honored."

"Nonsense," snapped His Excellency, "how could you be honored? It's too early in the morning to be honored, and at my age a man would like to sleep. Damn this thrice-damned code that drags us out before the sun itself!"

Coyote didn't know what to say, and therefore he kept still. It was something you learned early in his business; better to offend vaguely by saying nothing than to offend specifically by saying the wrong thing.

"In only three more years I will be retired, however," went on the Abban. "And then I shall sleep until nine

54

every morning and let the females of my household cluck about my senility all they want."

Coyote murmured the pleasantest murmur he had at his command, and the other man smiled, a smile of amazing elegance.

"Enough," said the Chief Legislator. "You have not come all the way from Mars-Central to listen to an old man complain. If you will come with me, they have set us breakfast on the balcony overlooking the river. I think you may find the view worth having risen early for."

They went out into the balcony and Coyote found himself in complete agreement with the Abban. The river sparkled in the morning light below them, not more than ten inches deep perhaps, foaming and frothing around boulders and pouring over low falls of rock. Occasionally a fish jumped, a pure arc of silver in the golden air. The balcony was alive with the flowers he had seen everywhere as they drove into the capitol, the air filled with their scent.

"It's very beautiful," Coyote said, sitting down across from the other man. "I am only sorry that I am here for business rather than pleasure."

His Excellency smiled. "Perhaps the pleasure will be more than you had expected," he said. "You have been given quarters here in the Palace, and you will not find it a dull place to live. A thaan-carriage has been put at your disposal, as well as a small flier. And there are, of course, the women; you will have to tell your valet when you go to your rooms just how many you will require, whether it is necessary that they be virgins, what your tastes are as to hair and eyes, and so on. I think you will find your business trip rather enjoyable."

Coyote sat speechless. How many women, eh? On wheat or on rye? With pickles or without? He shook his head, aware that the Abban was amused at his reaction.

"If I am not honored," he said finally, "I am at least overwhelmed."

The Chief Legislator laughed.

"Then let us get at once to business," he said briskly, "so that you may recover your equilibrium. You know our problem here?"

"Only in a broad, general way, Your Excellency. I

55

counted on people here to explain it all to me in more detail."

"Well, then. The problem is the Poet Jacinth. She is the third female Poet, only the third, in ten thousand years. That should tell you how rare such a creature is."

"How does a woman get to be a Poet?"

"It's relatively simple. She has only to send a message to someone at the University, on the Faculty of Poetry, signifying her intention to compete in the yearly Poetry Examinations."

"I see. And only three women have done so, in ten thousand years?"

"The examinations are given by computer, and they are extremely difficult. Of perhaps five thousand men who take them each year only a handful are accepted. For a woman even to compete—much less to do well—is a rare thing. I remember very few cases."

"And why is that? Since it is the only profession open to them I should think there would be many trying."

"Well," said His Excellency, "they are perhaps deterred by the penalty for failure."

"Penalty?"

"It's solitary confinement for life, Citizen Jones. A woman does not take such a prospect lightly. Very few compete."

Coyote concentrated, with some difficulty, on a bunch of pale pink grapes that reminded him of giant pearls. It would not do to lose his temper.

"Why such an incredible penalty?" he asked carefully. "It seems a little extreme."

"Perhaps it does," said the Abban, "until you consider it in context. No woman should attempt such a thing unless it is the will of the Holy Light, you see. If that is the case, of course she will pass, she cannot fail; if it is not, she is guilty of blasphemy, not to mention conduct unbecoming a female. And the disgrace is not just her own, she will have brought shame to her entire household, which may well number several hundred people. A severe penalty is unfortunately necessary, in order to prevent just the situation you describe—large numbers of bored females competing for Poetry just because they are allowed to do so."

"And the Poet Jacinth?" Coyote said. "She did pass?"

"At the Seventh Level. That is the most remarkable

thing of all, you see. Perhaps one percent of the men who attain the Major in Poetry reach this level. We have no higher position in our society than Poet of the Seventh Level . . . there is even a sense in which, repugnant though it may be, the Poet Jacinth outranks me also."

"And you hate her for it?"

The Abban looked at him with an expression that could not have been faked. Total, utter astonishment.

"Hate her?" he said. "Why?"

"Because she is a woman. And she outranks you."

"Oh, good heavens, Citizen Jones, of course I don't hate her. Nor does anyone else. She is not a woman like other women, she is holy, chosen of the Holy Light. As such she is very precious to us."

"To everyone?"

"With the exception of a few fanatics who either claim that she rigged the exams—a total impossibility—or prattle nonsense about purifying Poetry by removing her, she is universally beloved."

"Are these fanatics dangerous?"

"Not at all. They are idiots. They have parades, carry banners, that sort of thing. They're a nuisance, but harmless."

"I see." Coyote paused for a moment. "But someone, Your Excellency, someone is poisoning her."

"Yes. Why we cannot imagine. Even the poor benighted fools I mentioned would not want to harm her, only to banish her to her father's household. It's unthinkable that anyone should hurt her."

Coyote peeled a peach carefully and cut it into precise sections.

"You could explain to me, perhaps, why your own police could not handle this matter?"

"It is difficult to explain."

"Perhaps Your Excellency would try."

After a moment the Abban cleared his throat and spoke.

"As you say, I must try. You see, it is very difficult for us to deal with the Poet Jacinth in any way at all."

"Why?"

"It is a matter of rituals and taboos, my friend. The appropriate attitude to be taken by anyone, male or female, toward a Poet—especially at one of the high levels—is one of reverence, almost of subservience."

"Yes. Go on."

"The proper attitude to be taken toward a woman is very different indeed."

Coyote remembered the threedies of the women in their pens, lined up at the feeding troughs, with the brands livid on their hips and the heavy collars around their throats, and he could well believe that His Excellency spoke the truth. Things had changed, time had passed, since those threedies were taken, but nonetheless the situation was awkward. The mental habits of thousands of years cannot be discarded overnight, whatever the surface evidence.

"It must make for a certain conflict," he said.

"It does. It certainly does. There is no precedent for such a relationship, that of policeman and female Poet. And in our culture there is precedent, ritual, approved behavior, for every other situation. You see, Citizen, it is difficult for us. Our policemen simply cannot manage this particular case."

"Very well," said Coyote, "I will do the best I can."

"We are told that you are the finest agent the Tri-Galactic Intelligence Service has ever had."

Coyote dropped his eyes to his plate.

"I am honored," he murmured.

Chapter 3

It was incredible how much time one could waste on a planet with ten thousand years of recorded civilization. Coyote felt it might take five of the ten thousand just to develop the damned etiquette. The breakfast with the Chief of Law took a couple of hours, and then there was a brief interlude in the chapel of the Palace—obligatory—and then there was a tour, also obligatory, of the gardens. There was a discourse on the history of His Excellency's favorite mobile flowers, and another on the Earth-roses he had managed, at enormous expense, to develop here where it was alleged they could not be grown. By that time it was the hour for lunch, and there were plans already made for Coyote for that, and then there was the siesta—obligatory—that followed lunch, and by the time *that* was over it was halfway into the afternoon. Coyote was seething with frustration.

And even then it was to get worse before it got better. Every office he tried to reach by com-set was either closed or in the charge of a congenital idiot. Every call was a series of near-burlesque delays that he knew perfectly well were only the result of his not knowing the appropriate words to say to get him past the secretaries and lower officials, all of whom were human on Abba.

At last, completely defeated, he called the Serviceman in charge of his living quarters, explained that he was having difficulties, and requested that he be issued an interpreter.

"But the Citizen's command of Abban is superb! Not native, perhaps, but fluent, eloquent, nuanced! One would almost think the Citizen had learned Abban as a child!"

The Citizen's command of the how-dee-do's and the curtseys and the thankee-ma'am's is abominable," said Coyote grimly.

"Ah!" said the Abban. "Ah, yes! I see! Most wise, Citizen, most wise! If the Citizen would simply sit back and relax, make himself comfortable, it would be seen to. And at the same time, would the Citizen specify the women he wished sent to him?"

"Women?" For a moment Coyote was puzzled, and then he remembered. "Oh, yes, the women. Go ahead, send them, just get me an interpreter."

"How many women, Citizen?"

"Two."

"The Citizen's needs are modest," said the Abban admiringly.

"The Citizen is a very busy man," Coyote said.

"Of course, of course. And the physical characteristics, Citizen?"

"Characteristics?"

"Of the women. Tall? Short? Plump? Blue eyes?"

"Light's beard, I don't care! Pick me out whatever seems suitable and send them along. *And* the interpreter."

The Abban left, bowing and scraping, and Coyote spent what seemed to be interminable hours while nothing at all happened. The women arrived, which seemed a hopeful sign; at least there was now reason to believe that the Serviceman had not simply gone home to take a second siesta.

At last the com-set sounded two soft tones, and Coyote went to answer it.

It seemed that there would be a very slight delay—but only so very slight, surely the Citizen would be patient? Appointments were being made with all the people the Citizen wished to see, for the following day, beginning very early in the morning. An interpreter would be sent in plenty of time, suitably instructed, and the Citizen would find that everything would go smoothly.

Coyote cut it short.

"All right," he said wearily, "all right. This man will be here first thing in the morning—you promise me that?"

"We promise you."

"And if the Poet Jacinth should die of the poison tonight, or strangle in red tape—"

"I beg the Citizen's pardon?"

Coyote stared at the face in the com-set screen. It was a round fat face with a flourishing moustache and empty eyes. He decided he was wasting his time.

"Never mind," he told it. "Thank you for your help."

"Perhaps this evening the Citizen will take advantage of his unexpected leisure to explore our beloved city?"

"I doubt it," Coyote snapped. "I will probably go to bed early. I am exhausted with courtesy."

He mumbled his way through the requisite six lines of farewells and thumbed the TERMINATE button.

One of the women appeared with a tray of steaming food, her face—undoubtedly a beautiful face, Coyote had to give his Serviceman credit for that, at least—showing concern. She dropped to her knees before him with the tray, and waited, still with that silent frown troubling her eyes.

"What is your name, Citizeness?" Coyote asked.

"I am called Aletha," she said softly.

"Aletha. A pleasant name."

He reached over and took the tray from her, assuming that she would get to her feet, but she remained kneeling.

"Aletha?"

"Yes, Citizen?"

"Is something wrong?"

She looked at him for just a moment, long enough to give him a glimpse of lovely dark eyes, heavy-lashed and shaped like almonds, and then dropped her glance again.

"The Citizen is angry," she murmured.

"The Citizen is that. Yes."

"May I ask why?"

He tried to explain, eating the food as he went along. Aletha was joined by the other woman, also kneeling, and he tried explaining to her, too. So far as he could tell he got nowhere at all. Apparently they could not conceive of a life that was not punctuated with endless ritualized delays, even when another woman's life was endangered. The second woman, whose name was Josepha, even went so far as to hint that she was appalled by the idea of a life that was not circumscribed by a kind of court etiquette.

"How," she asked gently, "does one know what to do?"

Coyote gave it up, reminding himself that social reform not only was not his task but was forbidden to him, thanked them for the excellent dinner, and told them he was going out.

He took a map of Alsabaid and inserted it in the display slot of his com-set, pushing the PROJECT button. The map flashed onto the wall behind the set. He looked at it carefully. Let's see. He was in the Palace, facing out on the Kef Dibad, the Street of Law. Directly across the street was a small area of exotic shops offering wares from all over the Three Galaxies, running down to the banks of the river that surrounded the Jewel City. It was not the shop area that interested him, however.

He went to the window to look out, orienting himself again, and then turned back to the map to be sure.

Yes. It was dead ahead of him. He had only to go down into the Street of Law, cross it and follow the Kef ban-Feliz for perhaps three blocks, and he would come to the Vice Quarter, a small triangle that was bounded on one side by the shops, on the second by the wharves of Alsabaid's harbor, and on the third by the great river Lara, the River of Gold. Although why it should be called that was difficult to imagine, since all water on Abba was pale green.

The Vice Quarter of Abba had a certain noxious fame, even at the heart of the First Galaxy. He had not mentioned to the gentleman on the com-set that he intended to go there, because he knew there would have been protests, and probably a companion forced upon him to prevent any ticklish intergalactic incidents. But it was in Vice Quarters, on planets which would tolerate them, that one learned things—if there was anything to learn.

He turned off the projection, pulled a light gray cloak from his gear and slipped it over his head, and went out into the corridors of the Palace of Law. The gray cloak was enough like the garments worn by the members of the Profession of Business that he felt it might very well get him by; certainly in the darkness of the Vice Quarter there would at least be a chance that he would draw little attention. And if he was challenged, of course, he had only to show his off-world credit disk, and everyone would at once begin to carry on about how honored they were.

He waved away the Serviceman who came forward at the end of each corridor to greet him, as well as the one who leaped up at the outside door. There could not, he thought, possibly be any unemployment on Abba. A place for everyone and everyone in his place.

"A walk," he told the man at the door. "Air, to clear my head after my long trip."

The Serviceman smiled and bowed. "You would not perhaps prefer the thaan-carriage which has been set aside for you, Citizen? You might lose your way in these streets at night."

"No, thank you," said Coyote. "If I lose my way I'll ask someone for directions. I prefer to walk."

"That pleasure rush to meet you, then, Citizen," said the Serviceman respectfully. "It is a beautiful night. The *halfa* are in bloom."

The Serviceman pointed. "See there, Citizen? On the balcony across the street?"

Coyote followed the pointing finger with his eyes. Down from the balcony hung a thick tangle of vines, swaying gently in the soft wind off the river. The flowers spread great yellow disks the size of saucers, flecked subtly at the heart with deepest purple.

"Very lovely," said Coyote approvingly.

"Thank you, Citizen," the Serviceman answered. "They bloom only during this month; the Citizen is fortunate."

Coyote moved out into the night, crossed the street, and to distract the Serviceman, who he knew was watching, he wandered down the street of shops, pausing to peer into the windows like any tourist, waiting for an opportunity to slip out of the man's line of vision. He found it at the fourth storefront, where a narrow arcade of pale rose tile ran back into the heart of the block, with display windows down both sides and a tiny garden down the middle.

He turned into this and went quickly down the arcade, coming out on the other side of the block safely beyond the Serviceman's eyes, on the Kef ban-Feliz.

He smelled the Vice Quarter before he saw it. Perfumes, incense burning in braziers, fountains with scented water spraying the night, cheap restaurant cooking the Light only knew what. And then he saw it and stopped to stare. It was something to see. Not just the shops and buildings; they were odd, to be sure, since no planet that

Coyote knew of in the inner two galaxies had had open display windows for over five hundred years. To buy something from a store on Mars-Central you dialed its number on your com-set, requested a goods display, watched the photographs of things to buy until you saw what you wanted, placed the order, and in perhaps fifteen minutes the selected items arrived at your door by roboconveyer.

But what held Coyote's interest was an enormous tree of some crystal plastic, rising perhaps three stories into the air and spreading its limbs out over an entire block. From every branch there hung the opaque spheres of campingbubbles, in every conceivable color, so that the whole effect was something like a giant Christmas tree flung up by someone with adominable taste. The bubbles were not to look at, though; as Coyote watched, a private flier pulled up at one of them and a man leaned out and tapped gently upon its side. At once the opacity became translucence and Coyote saw the slender woman within, arranged for maximum sales appeal upon a bed that filled the small, round room. The man looked, also, apparently was not satisfied with what he saw, and shook his head; immediately the bubble went opaque again.

Coyote chuckled. What a way to run a whorehouse, after all! This arrangement must be for the benefit of tourists, travelers in from the excursion rockets, students, men too poor to have households of their own, and the like.

There was a soft sound beside him; it turned into the usual train of remarks about what the Citizen might desire and how our humble planet was honored to have the Citizen aboard, and Coyote gritted his teeth and pulled a smile out of his intergalactidiplomatic hat.

"I, too, am honored, Citizen," he said to the man who had moved to walk beside him. "I am immeasurably honored. The significance of all previous experiences pales beside——"

The Abban chuckled and raised his hand in a cuttingoff gesture that was pangalactic.

"Careful, Citizen," he said with amusement. "If you get too good at that no one will believe you are an offworlder, and without the robes of a Criminal it would go hard with you to be carrying a faked off-world credit disk.

65

"The *smile* didn't even convince me. You come from a more rough-and-ready planet, a place where business comes before pleasure, if pleasure ever comes at all. You find it difficult to be patient with all our manners' claptrap. Fine. I am an adaptable man. We will dispense with all of that. What brings you to the Ruby Ring, Citizen? What can I do for you?"

The Ruby Ring, eh? Coyote smiled, a real smile this time. The name was apt. He looked at the man who strode easily at his side. The Abban wore the lavender robe of the professional criminal, and although he was a very tall man, even taller than Coyote, and skeletally thin, with the stooped bearing of one who is accustomed to having to continually bend over to hear and to be heard, he walked with grace. About his forehead were looped strands of beads, braided in fours, and in his nostrils he wore a ring of ivory. He was an imposing man, obviously a man secure in his position and that position one of power.

"Well, Citizen? Can I help you in any way? Is it a woman that you need?"

"Oh, no," said Coyote, "not a woman."

"A man, then?"

"I prefer women."

"Perhaps you have a wife at home, my friend, very fresh and new, still preferred above all others—that doesn't last, of course, but it's nice while it's going on."

"No. I've no wife. No wife and no women."

The Abban made a soft, sympathetic noise.

"And you don't want one. You must have been sadly mistreated by some female, Citizen."

"Mmm . . . not exactly," Coyote said, rather taken with the man and his talk, especially since he himself was being expertly guided, seemingly without any deliberate intent, straight toward the heart of the quarter. What sort of establishment might the fellow have there, he wondered?

"No," Coyote went on, "I haven't been mistreated. I'm afraid I'm one of the stupid ones where women are concerned. There was a woman I should have appreciated. Unfortunately she asked for nothing, and so that was exactly what I gave her. I talked a lot of garbage about having no ties, not that she had tried to create any. And then one day she was gone and I realized that being without her was unpleasant."

"It had never occurred to you before?"

"Not once."

"Like the air," said the Abban. "You certainly don't appreciate the stuff, but if the supply is cut off, the discomfort is striking."

"Exactly like that," said Coyote.

"I see. And by the way I am not—I repeat, I am not—leading you to my personal place of business as you think I am."

A small warning bell rang in Coyote's head.

"You are a telepath, then?" he asked.

"Well, of course," said the Abban. "How could one be a Criminal without being telepathic?"

Coyote immediately activated his own shields and the Abban smiled acknowledgment.

"I see," he said, and inclined his head on its long bony stem of neck. "You, too."

"You specialize in what?" asked Coyote. "Murder? Rape? Arson? Forgery?"

"None of those."

"What, then?"

"Poison, of course."

"Ah," Coyote said. "That's why you came to me!"

"Precisely."

"And where are we going?"

"To a man who knows everything there is to know about poisons."

They had turned a corner and were in an open square filled with transparent bubbles where legitimate goods were on display, and Coyote assumed anything at all, legal or illegal, could probably be purchased. The Abban took Coyote's elbow and led him a winding way among the bubbles. The smell of spice and flowers was choking; Coyote ducked his head in a futile attempt to escape the overpowering burden of perfume borne by the air. On his left he saw a threedie house, advertising incredibly ingenious combinations—of salaciousness. What would a Mars-turtle be doing as a sexual act with a Venusian flame-tiger, for the Light's sake?

Ahead of them was a sort of labyrinth of arcades, dim archways leading down past doors through which he could glimpse people moving, a whirl of many-colored robes in the dimness. They entered one of these paths along with a pack of shoving tourists and Abbans; through a triangular window in a wall beside him Coyote saw a circle of people crouched with their foreheads touching while a single light flashed blinding silver again and again in their center.

"What are they doing?" he asked his guide.

The man shrugged. "A cult," he said. "We have cults for every taste here. Jehovans. Satan-worshippers. Hifeedists. Deep Night Dancers. Mescalists. Swordswallowing Fundamentalists. You name it, we've got it. Ah, here we are!"

"Here" was a dark and narrow doorway, in which both Coyote and the Abban had to stoop.

"Sorry, my friend," said the Abban. "This part of the city is eight thousand years old, and we were a shorter people when it was built. Duck—there you are."

Coyote looked around him, blinking even in the dimness, the entry had been so very dark. It was a kind of café, apparently; at least there were small, low tables surrounded by piled cushions. The Abban took him over to a table set in a niche in the brick wall of the place. Two more Abbans sat there, relaxed on the cushions, both in the lavender robes of Crime.

"Marcus? White-Eyes?" said the Abban, addressing them, Coyote noted happily, without all the usual preliminary formulas. "Here he is, Coyote Jones, come all the way from Mars-Central to learn about the poisoners of Abba."

How much did he know? Coyote wondered behind his shields, and then had to laugh at himself. He was not accustomed to being sent on missions that were a matter of public knowledge; the cloak-and-dagger response was automatic.

"Well done, Neo," said the one he had called Marcus. "Sit down, Citizen Jones; we have already ordered for you. Now tell us, since Neo has brought you to experts, what we can tell *you* about the poison and poisoners. Is there a specific question?"

Marcus smiled, White-Eyes—whose eyes were very brown—smiled, Neo smiled, Coyote smiled. Coyote was amazed. He could hardly wait to get back and tell Tzana about the whole thing. The ingenuity of it all . . . a planet where crime was legal! Then what would real crime be? Or could there be a real crime?

"The Citizen is shielded," murmured White-Eyes, and the others nodded, and they all smiled some more.

"Your questions, Citizen?" Marcus prodded gently.

A Serviceman came and set their drinks in front of them, steaming pale blue liquid in little crystal cups.

"I am here to investigate the poisoning of the Poet Jacinth," said Coyote, sipping his drink. It was excellent. And then the thought hit him, a little too late.

"Is this drink poisoned?" he asked stupidly, watching the room whirl around him, watching White-Eyes double and merge, flow into Marcus, watching Neo elongate and spread across the cushions, watching the dark become a tunnel in front of his eyes, and then he knew nothing more.

Chapter 4

The taste in his mouth was beyond belief. If he had been psi-kinetic he could have at least removed the slime that coated his teeth; as it was, he gulped air, hoping that would help. It didn't.

He was in a tiny room, he lay on a pile of straw on the floor, and he was expertly bound. Cords circled his ankles and wrists and throat, intricately knotted so that any attempt at movement forced him to choke himself. Very nice.

He was disgusted with himself; after all, what would be the business of professional poisoners on Abba? To poison, naturally. He would have been wiser to have stayed on Mars-Central and sent Ratha on the assignment. *She* would have been too smart to fall for that cup-of-tea-in-a-cozy-nook bit.

He tried to roll over, and the building, whatever it was, swayed alarmingly beneath him. His stomach lurched and he fought back the bile that threatened to foul his already stinking nest. In such close quarters the last thing he needed was a puddle of his own vomit. Although if he had to stay here long there were bound to be puddles of one kind or another.

He lay still and studied his surroundings. The floor seemed to be rough synthowood beneath the straw. There was no door, as far as he could tell, only a single window high in the wall. They must have chucked him through it already trussed like a bird for roasting. The walls slanted

70

up to a near-point . . . the building would have to have roughly the shape of a beehive. For a large and very stupid bee who had come straight to the nectar laid out for him. The place was very dirty, it could not have been used recently, but where was it? The swaying bit bothered him. For all he knew he was suspended by a thread over a precipice, or floating around in an ocean full of the Abban equivalent of sharks. Anything was possible. He was going to have to get to that window and look out, somehow, if he could keep from strangling in the process.

He ignored the sickening movement of the structure, rolled as carefully as he dared until he lay directly beneath the window, and then took a long breath and held it. The air in his lungs held him just long enough for the single lunge to his feet, and then he fell with a bone-shattering crash to the floor again. It was fortunate that he had been able to get a glimpse of the situation in that one try, because he could not have made a second one. The muscles of his neck felt as if they had been crushed, and everything else—legs, back, arms, chest—was in agony.

He rested without moving until the building ceased to sway and the room stopped exploding with circles of red and black before his eyes, and then considered the situation. He had had only a glimpse, but the glimpse had been sufficient. There was no precipice involved, no sharks, no ocean. This structure he was in, whatever it was, was perched on slender poles in the middle of a river. Muddy green water stretched in all directions around it, and in the distance, almost out of sight, was the city of Alsabaid.

Damn. He was going to miss all those interviews. They would probably cancel the interpreter and it would turn out that there was some regulation limiting him to one application-for-interpreter per Abban year. The Poet Jacinth would be dead before he ever got started investigating. This was where curiosity got you. Tzana Kai had pointed that out to him once.

"Curiosity," she had said flatly, "is useful only when it is an intellectual vice. When it becomes a matter of the passions, as it is with you, it ceases to be simply a tool of the mind and becomes a way of getting oneself killed."

She had pointed it out to him only once; Tzana never pointed anything out twice.

And he had had no chance whatsoever, in all the time

he'd spent here in this hyperorganized pseudo-Arabian-Nights, to find out anything at all about the thing his curiosity had lured him here to investigate—that is, what a docile, subordinate, underdog woman was like. If he had stayed home last night—he hoped it was only last night, and assumed it to be, since he had no puddles of any variety to deal with as yet—if he *had* stayed home and satisfied his curiosity on *that* particular matter, he wouldn't be in this mess now. That was where devotion to bloody *duty* got you!

He wasn't in any danger, of course. Unless the poles broke and threw him into the water, where he would no doubt drown, tied up as he was. But that wasn't likely. The problems that faced him at this moment were protocol-type problems.

Mass projective telepathy, his only talent, was just the thing for a situation like this. He had only to shape a thought—GET THE BLINKING HELL OUT TO THE RIVER AND GET ME OUT OF THIS STUPID HUT— and head it Alsabaid-ward. Inside of ten minutes there would have been a hundred people knocking each other down to rescue him and a thousand behind them trying to help. But that would be very bad form indeed. If it became known to all of Alsabaid that he was not just a rather bumbling TGIS agent with a long red beard and a minor talent for shielding against other people's telepathic probing, if it became known that he could handle hundreds of people at a time just by thinking at them, it would be a ninety days' wonder, all Three Galaxies would know about it in a week's time, and he'd be no more use to the Tri-Galactic Intelligence Service.

For a moment that certain result almost tempted him, particularly when he thought of the helpless rage of the Fish in such a situation. But there were also personal consequences of being a Tri-Galactic marvel. He'd have no privacy ever again. Everywhere he went people would get out of his way, fast, and hide behind things and point and go "There-goes-the-famous-mass-projective-telepath." He didn't want that to happen.

No, it wouldn't do. He would just have to wait until some person or some group of no more than two or three persons came by. He could manage to get one or two people to come out here, rescue him, get him to shore, and then convince them that they hadn't done anything of the kind, without any troublesome results.

Although of course it might be a couple of weeks before anybody came out this way.

Coyote sighed. It was all very inconvenient. Perhaps on the next assignment he could convince them to send someone along to take care of him, since he apparently couldn't manage for himself.

In the meantime, what could he do?

He couldn't review the problem, because until he could get to the interviews with the police and the officials at the Temple of Poetry he didn't have anything to review.

He could think about Bess, but that would be embarrassing. Ratha's mother had been a revolutionary, a guerrilla fighter—and she had always gotten away, until the day she chose to turn herself in for her own very excellent reasons. She would never have found herself in a situation like this.

He could sleep. That seemed the most sensible course, if he didn't die of the taste in his mouth before he woke up. Whatever the poison had been, its basic ingredient must have been rotted fish.

He relaxed as much as he could, closed his eyes, sighed again, and waited. A blank mind in a blank body, he told himself. Sure sign of health.

What was that thing the Maklunites had taught him that would put you to sleep? He stirred around in his memory a bit, wishing he had a few of those gentle, loving people to keep him company while he waited—although he wouldn't have breathed at them, in his condition—and it came back to him. Fifteen syllables, carefully chosen for harmony, euphony, rhythm. Imagine them on a string, each syllable a small, serene sphere unto itself. Fasten the two ends of the string together and go round and round and round and round. . . .

It was almost dark when he woke up again, miserable, aching, half-starved, and with a bursting bladder. The sound of a movement on the river below had wakened him, as he had known it would; now it was time.

He gathered his thought carefully and headed it out in the general direction of the sound, not too powerfully, and not for long. This was harder, actually, than blasting a crowd of people into doing what he wanted, because he had to be so careful. Just enough and not too much, and unless they had set a constant telepathic watch on him, someone good to whom distance was irrelevant, he could be reasonably sure of getting away with it.

THERE IS SOMEONE IN THE BUILDING WHO NEEDS HELP, he projected carefully. THERE IS SOMEONE IN THE BUILDING WHO NEEDS HELP.

The sound outside, the sound that had been a steady, rhythmic interruption of the water, suddenly stopped.

THERE IS SOMEONE IN THE BUILDING. WHO NEEDS HELP, Coyote repeated, adding to himself, "You thick-headed ass." How long was it going to take him?

He felt the hut shudder violently, and then the failing light from the window was cut off altogether as someone peered through the opening at him.

"Hello, there?" said a voice uncertainly. "May the Light shine upon you? Is someone there?"

"Only me," said Coyote, amazed at how tired he was. "Only me and the ropes I'm tied up with."

"What can I do?" asked Someone. "There's no door to this thing . . . you're tied up . . . I don't know how to get you out."

"Do you have a knife with you? Something to cut with?"

"I have a fishing knife."

"Then throw it over to me—no, wait. If you throw too hard it may go somewhere where I can't get to it. Tie something to it, a piece of string, your sash, whatever, a piece of fishing-line. Then throw it."

Almost at once there was the clatter of metal on the bare floor of the hut, and Coyote swore.

"I meant," he said carefully, "for you to hold the other end of the line you tied it to, friend. The point was that you could then pull it back and throw it again, if necessary."

"I'm sorry. I'm very sorry," said the Someone. "I didn't think. I am a plain man. I have never done anything like this before."

"Never mind," said Coyote. "You did fine, actually. The knife landed an inch from my throat and I can reach it easily."

"Oh. I am sorry."

"And I," said Coyote, cutting the last cord, "am honored."

"You are honored?" The voice was full of wonder, and Coyote left it that way.

"How are you staying at the window like that? he asked. "Can you fly?"

"No. no. There's a ladder here. Awfully shaky, but a ladder. It goes right up to the window."

"And below? Do you have a boat down there?"

"Yes, Citizen. A small boat, but it will bear our weight."

Coyote let out his breath slowly. This was going to be easy after all. Only one man, and a small boat.

"Look here," he said as he tested his cramped muscles, "your boat may be able to take both our weights but that ladder won't. You climb down and get your boat to the foot of the ladder and I'll follow you, all right?"

His legs were full of needles and the situation in his shoulder muscles didn't bear thinking of. He would probably fall off the ladder, hit his head on the boat, and kill himself. Like the ancient folk-hero, Big Guthrie, who had hit himself over the head with a toilet seat and knocked himself unconscious.

"Are you coming? Are you all right?"

"I'm fine," Coyote shouted back to the voice from below. It was a flat-out lie, but he had a certain amount of professional pride. He staggered over to the window on legs he could not feel and looked out to make sure about the ladder. There it was; old, rickety, and likely to pull the hut down when he put his weight on it. Nevertheless . . .

"Be careful, Citizen," said the guy with the boat, superfluously.

Coyote went down the ladder in one rush, feeling that if he was going to simply fall off it into the boat, which was the most likely thing, he might just as well look as if he wasn't worried about that possibility. If he did fall it would look as if he'd overestimated his abilities, but if he didn't he'd look peaches and roses.

And he made it. The boat rocked alarmingly, and the poor man, who wore the robes of Service, kept looking at him with unhealthy suspicion, but they made it to shore and stepped out on the banks just a hundred yards from the outskirts of Alsabaid.

THERE WAS NOBODY IN THE BUILDING. EVERYTHING HAS BEEN PERFECTLY ORDINARY TODAY, Coyote projected very carefully as the man pulled away. NOBODY WAS IN THE BUILDING, NOTHING HAPPENED. YOU HAVE BEEN FISHING, NOTHING UNUSUAL HAPPENED.

He watched the man's back get smaller, satisfied that that would do it. And then a bony hand clapped him on the shoulder and a voice said enthusiastically, "Well done, Citizen Jones! Well done!"

He whirled around, doing more violence to his bruised body, and there stood Neo, like an El Greco fanatic in lavender, and a smaller flier beside him.

"Well done?" he asked. It sounded feeble, but it was all he could say.

"Yes, indeed," said Neo. "It's been a pleasure dealing with you, I must say. But enough of this shop talk, I know you're tired and miserable—let me give you a ride back to the old Law shack, all right?"

When they were in the flier and headed toward the Palace of Law, at a satisfying speed for once, Coyote asked Neo a question.

"My friend," he said, with no sarcasm intended—after all, it had only been a man doing his job—"would you answer a question about Abban poisons now? Without poisoning me again, that is?"

"Gladly," said Neo. "One question, free of charge. What is it?"

"Is there a posion on Abba, as far as you know, that can be introduced into food or drink, leave no trace whatsoever, but cause violent pain about thirty minutes after ingestion? Without being fatal, that is?"

"Certainly," said Neo. "I can think of a dozen that would do that. However, they would all be fatal eventually; that is, the effects are cumulative."

"No trouble for someone to find such a thing, though?"

"None at all," said Neo cheerfully.

He set the flier down expertly at the curb in front of the Palace and let Coyote out.

"It's been a genuine pleasure dealing with you, Citizen," he said again, as he took off. "A very genuine pleasure. A lot of people die from that stuff we gave you."

"They don't die from the poison," Coyote told him with

great relish. "You're flattering yourself. What they die from is the lack of a toothbrush afterwards."

He turned on his heel and left the poisoner laughing at the curb, swept, with what he hoped was dignity, past the Servicemen posted in door and niches, and made it to his rooms.

Just in time.

Chapter 5

When he had made himself respectable once again, Coyote went through the rooms looking for the two women who had been sent to him. He was hungry and assumed they might well be hungry, too, and for all he knew they could not eat unless he ordered the food for them.

"Aletha?" he called. "Josepha? Citizenesses? Where are you?"

A figure rose from his couch and bowed. He wore the insignia of the Women's Discipline Unit.

"Good evening, Citizen Jones," he said. "We have been wondering where you were. I am Kidj ban-Kidj, at your service."

"I was unavoidably detained," said Coyote curtly.

"Well," said ban-Kidj, "you would insist on going to the Ruby Ring, Citizen. I'm afraid your unpleasant experience in the river hut is entirely due to your own lack of wisdom."

"Oh, you know all about it, then? The poisoning, the dumping in that miserable hut, all that stuff?"

"Of course, Citizen. Neo ban-Valdeverl is a respectable man; the crime was registered with the Palace of Law immediately upon its completion."

Coyote stopped dead in his tracks.

"You mean to tell me," he shouted, "that you people *knew* what had happened to me, and you didn't send anyone to help me?"

Ban-Kidj raised his eyebrows.

"Citizen Jones," he said, "if the result of registration of crimes were immediate interference by the Law, the profession of Crime would die out in a year. Criminals have certain rights, too, you know, and they are respected."

"But in that case," Coyote demanded, "what are the police *for?*"

"They are very busy men," said ban-Kidj. "They have to keep track of the crimes, everything must be accounted for. It is necessary to be certain that all forms have been filled out, all fees paid, all regulations conformed with. And then they protect us, of course, from crimes committed by scum who are not members of the criminal profession."

Coyote sat down wearily. There was absolutely nothing he could think of to say or to do. The whole thing was mad. The Fish had told him not to expect barbarians, and he had been quite right; the thing to expect on Abba was raving lunatics.

"Where," he asked finally, in the weariest voice he'd heard in many a day, "are my good friends Aletha and Josepha? I would like them to join me for dinner. And incidentally, where is my interpreter?"

Ban-kidj bowed again. "The interpreter was provided, as agreed, and he kept your appointments for you. The transcripts of the interviews, very complete in their details, very satisfactory, I am sure, are in the red folder on your desk there. Verbatim. The interpreter was accompanied by a secretary."

"Good," said Coyote. "I'll read them right after dinner. Have I appointments for tomorrow?"

"You are to see the Poet Jacinth herself, Citizen. At nine o'clock."

"Good, good. If she lives through the night. And the women?"

"Women, Citizen?"

"Aletha and Josepha. Where are they, do you know?"

"Why, they have been taken away, Citizen."

Coyote sat up straight. Something in the tone of the fellow's voice didn't strike him as quite what it should be. For the perhaps two millionth time he regretted the fact that he was only a projective telepath and not a receptive as well.

79

"What do you mean, exactly?" he asked cautiously. "Taken away where? And why?"

"They have been taken to the nearest Women's Discipline Unit for punishment, Citizen. We certainly have no intention of neglecting your rights in any way, however. Nothing has been done to them, pending your notification as to what sort of punishment you wish inflicted."

Coyote took a deep breath. He felt as if he were under water.

"Ban-Kidj," he said softly, "please explain. Please grope around in the depths of your bureaucratic brain and explain to me why those two women are to be punished."

Ban-Kidj regarded him with bland, wondering eyes.

"Why, for the usual reasons, Citizen," he said.

"Explain!" Coyote thundered.

"They did not please you, Citizen; therefore they must be punished."

"How do you know that they did not please me? Did I complain?"

"They reported in this morning, as it was their duty to do," said ban-Kidj. "They are excellent females, well trained and eager to do what they are told. They were honored to be chosen to serve a person as important as yourself. I am amazed, myself, that you found them unsatisfactory—however, that is your right."

"But, look, Citizen," said Coyote, straining for comprehension, "how can they know or you know if I was or wasn't pleased with them? I haven't had a chance to find *out* if I was pleased, for the Light's sake!"

"Exactly," said ban-Kidj, as though that settled it. "Exactly."

Coyote sat and thought a minute. The idea that came to him was intolerable.

"What did these two criminals report to you this morning?" he asked carefully. "What, exactly?"

"They are not criminals, Citizen, they are females. Females have no sense of right or wrong and therefore cannot commit crimes. They simply called in, as they are required to do, and told us that you had not so much as touched either one of them."

"But I haven't even been here!"

"Citizen Jones," said ban-Kidj, "if you had been pleased

with them you would not have gone out into the Vice Quarter."

Coyote buried his head in his hands until he was able to talk once again.

"Do I have this straight," he asked finally, "do I have this exactly right? Neo and Marcus and what's-his-name—White-Eyes—can poison me, tie me up, and abandon me to die in a hut in the middle of the river. That's all right with everyone, that's their Profession, and we must concern ourselves with their due rights and privileges. But those two poor women, just because I—who am here to find a poisoner, I remind you, not to take part in orgies—just because I did not leap on those two women and take advantage of the facilities, so to speak, they are to be punished?"

"A very good analysis of the situation, Citizen Jones," said ban-Kidj with approval. "You see things very clearly. And if you will just give me instructions I will go at once to the com-set and let the Unit know what punishment you have ordered for the women. And then, of course, I will see that you are sent two replacements at once."

Coyote came out of the chair with a single movement and took ban-Kidj by the collar of his robe, lifting the elegant official right off the floor and into the air.

"You will not!" he bellowed. "You will do nothing of the kind! You will take me—at once—this instant—to wherever you have shut up Aletha and Josepha, who please me, very much, do you hear? And you will release them to me and I will bring them back here, where I will damn well just sit and *look* at them if that happens to be what I want to do! Do you understand me? Either you will do that or I will tear down your accursed Women's Discipline Unit, synthobrick by synthobrick, until I find them!"

He set the man down on the floor with a thud and hit him right between the eyes with a thought that turned ban-Kidj as green as the River of Gold.

"Yes, Citizen," said ban-Kidj in a hasty gargle. "At once, Citizen. If you will just come with me, Citizen. We are honored, of course, to carry out the Citizen's wishes."

"You are accursed!" shouted Coyote. "Honored bemdung! Hurry up!"

"The Citizen does not wish to eat first?"

81

Coyote fixed him with a glance that froze him to the spot.

"All right," said ban-Kidj, raising his hands imploringly. "If the Citizen will follow me."

The Women's Discipline Unit was a circular building, cut up into sections like a pie, with a central business office at the hub of the circle full of computers and robots and men in dark blue robes. Ban-Kidj and Coyote went through it like a whirlwind, gathering astonished looks as they passed, Coyote driving the Abban before him like a terrified steer.

Ban-Kidj took him to a round door with a number of studs set into it. Then he began punching out various combinations of the studs, which lit up in different colors, red, yellow, and green, as he touched them.

"What are you doing?" Coyote demanded.

"I am sending a message through," said ban-Kidj with a quaver. "I am having Three-oh-nine-one and One-four-four-four sent down here to us at once."

"Three-oh-nine-one and One-four-four-four? What is that?"

"The two women, Citizen. They are numbered, of course, for the convenience of the Unit. You realize, surely, that there are hundreds of Alethas and Josephas in this district, you realize——"

He was interrupted by the sounding of a small bell, and the door slid open. Behind it was another door, equally massive, and in the space between the two doors stood Aletha and Josepha. Apparently, whatever horrors lay behind that door, he was not going to get a glimpse of them.

The two women were white and trembling, it hurt him just to look at them. He counted to ten, reminding himself that he must not offend the citizens of this very powerful planet that paid so large a sum of taxes, may they all—the males, anyway—boil in eternal oil, and spoke to the women.

"Are you all right?" he asked them.

They dropped at once to the floor and hid their faces on their knees.

"What the devil have they done to them?" Coyote demanded. "I have given no instructions as to the type of

82

punishment and you had no right to take action without such instructions!"

"Nothing has been done to them," said ban-Kidj, who had become a great deal more virile now that he had two females watching him. "Don't be ridiculous, Citizen, we know the law. They are simply ashamed."

"Ashamed of what?"

"Of having displeased you, of course."

With hearty contempt in his voice, he added, "As they certainly should be."

The two women winced and caught their breath, and Coyote longed for the freedom to kill the WDU man.

"Aletha?" he said instead. "Josepha? I have come to take you back with me. Ban-Kidj here is anxious to go make arrangements for transportation. We are going to have a pleasant dinner together, just the three of us."

He pulled the two of them, unbelieving and protesting that such things could not happen on Abba, to their feet, and he took them to the front entrance as rapidly as he had brought ban-Kidj to the door of the rooms where they were being kept. A small flier waited for them there, fitted out with heavy black curtains to hide the women from view as they flew. Coyote gave it a vicious kick with the toe of his sandal.

"Get in, please," he told the women.

They stared at him and he opened the flier door and repeated, "Get in. Please. I would be honored if you would go back with me to the Palace of Law."

He had about as much sexual interest in these two poor cowed creatures as he had in the flier, probably less, but nobody was going to get punished because he hadn't laid them, not as long as he was conscious and in full possession of his private parts. They would have dinner, and perhaps an hour's sleep, and then, sore muscles or no sore muscles, he would get to the business of providing Aletha and Joseph with proper references for *their* next assignment.

Aletha and Josepha lay sleeping, finally, with their various emotional injuries as satisfactorily repaired as he had been able to manage. Coyote gave them a glance of inspection and ticked it off—two females, one brunette, one blond, both asleep, breathing deep and slow, cheeks

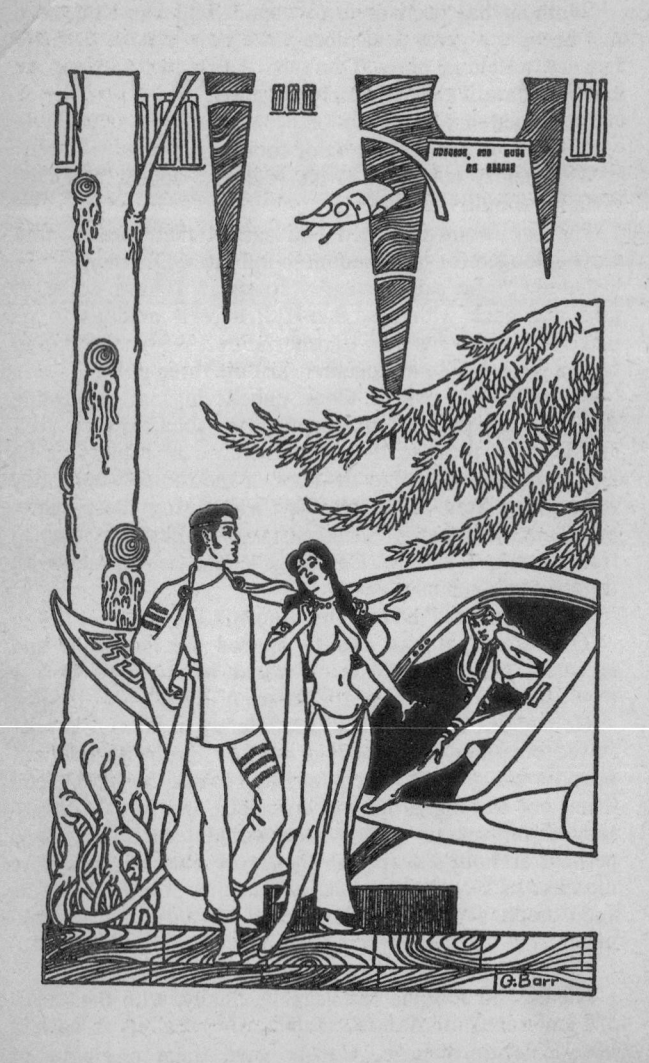
G.Barr

charmingly flushed, no sign of tension on either face. Check.

He went out into the main room of the suite, trying not to stagger, and picked up the folder of transcribed interviews from the desk. He sat up to read them, since he knew he could not possibly stay awake if he lay down, and at that the print kept swimming out of focus before his eyes. He went to the bath and put his head under a stream of cold water until he felt capable of keeping his eyes open, wondering if he wasn't perhaps getting too old for this work, then went back and settled down with what looked to be the most informative report, the one from the police.

Q: You are Helix, of the household of Min, member at the Fifth Level of the Profession of Law, police division. Is that correct?

A: That is correct.

Q: And you have been handling the investigation of the attempted poisoning of the Poet Jacinth?

A: Yes. At least, I have been trying to do so. It is rather complicated by the problems of procedure.

Q: I understand. Very well. What is the usual location of these poison attempts?

A: Well, the Poet Jacinth, of course, lives in the Trance Cloister of the Temple of Poetry. She usually takes her evening meal in her own rooms, on the second floor of the Cloister. She then goes into a small garden, which is her favorite place for meditation, and spends perhaps two or three hours there, and that's when it happens.

Q: Is she attended during her meal?

A: She has a servingwoman with her.

Q: When do the effects of the poison first appear usually?

A: Generally from thirty minutes to an hour after the Poet Jacinth has completed her meal.

Q: At that time she would be in the garden?

A: That is correct, yes.

Q: And what are the usual effects? Vomiting, or convulsions, or——

A: There has never been any vomiting. It is always exactly the same. The Poet Jacinth will be kneeling in deep meditation, perfectly tranquil. Suddenly she will gasp and fall to the ground as if she had been struck. She describes the pain as being primarily confined to her head and says that if it were not that it is of such brief duration it would certainly kill her, so intense is it.

Q: I see. How long does this go on?

A: Apparently what it amounts to is repeated impulses of this pain, each impulse extremely brief, but with only short intervals of relief in between. At first it generally continued for no more than five minutes or so, but recently the length of the attacks has been increasing. Last night the Poet had to endure almost an hour of the pain, and this morning she is very ill and despondent as a result. She feels that she cannot possibly stand very much more of it.

Q: Does this occur every night, without exception?

A: No. At one time, three nights passed without any such occurrence.

Q: And how long has this been going on?

A: About four weeks, Citizen.

Q: What measures have you taken for the protection of the Poet? What investigations have been made?

A: The things you would expect. Routine. We have changed the persons who prepare her food. We have changed the location of that preparation and had it all prepared under the uninterrupted surveillance of other Poets and our own men. Still, somehow, the poison is put into the food. Whoever is responsible is unbelievably clever.

Q: Perhaps it is the Poet's servingwoman? Have you considered that?

A: Of course. We're not fools here, you know, Citizen. We've changed servingwomen—much against the Poet Jacinth's will, since she was deeply attached to the old one. We've set every conceivable guard, set watches everywhere throughout the Temple, tried every combination of safeguards our best men could devise. It makes no difference, still the poisoning goes on. The doctors are seriously alarmed . . .

Q: No one else has been affected?
A: No one. Only the Poet herself.
Q: Do you know of any reason why anyone would want to harm her?
A: None whatsoever.
Q: Very strange. The food has been analyzed, I suppose?
A: Of course. Numerous times.
Q: And the results?
A: There were no results.
Q: I don't understand.
A: There has never been any detectable poison in the food or drink. This is not surprising, however, since the poisoners are extremely clever at devising new combinations with which our chemists are not familiar. It is, of course, an unregistered crime, you must remember, or we would know what poison was invloved—not that any respectable Criminal would harm a Poet, female or not.
Q: I understand. Well, then, perhaps we had best leave the next step to Citizen Jones. He has had a great deal more experience in dealing with this sort of thing than I have.
A: So we have heard. And you will be assisting Citizen Jones in the future?
Q: I expect to do so, although at the moment the Citizen is having some minor difficulties.
A: I hope that he is able to resolve them satisfactorily. We can't afford to have this sort of thing going on, it leads to a lack of confidence in the police.
Q: I wouldn't worry.

They wouldn't worry, eh? The agent they had requested stuffed full of drugs, tied up and abandoned to die, but not to worry. It being a registered crime.

Coyote glanced through the other transcripts, which did little more than recapitulate the one he had already read, and then flung the folder across the room in disgust and went to sleep where he lay.

Chapter 6

Coyote stood uncomfortably in the room where the student had brought him and waited. For this interview the interpreter had refused to help him.

"I would have far more difficulty in dealing with the Poet Jacinth than you would, Citizen," the Abban had insisted. "You have no taboos to hamper you. And as for ritual and precedent, in this case there *is* none. You will handle it better without me there, nervous and confused, hampering you."

They had dressed him in a blue tunic and sandals, his hair was caught back with a clasp of hammered silver set with amethysts, and over the tunic in an elaborate drape he wore a robe of deepest purple, made of the silken fur of the hela-foxes of Abba. He carried a silver staff bearing the insignia of the Palace of Law, it having been decided that this was closest to his professional status, and around his neck swung an ankh of a rare lavender metal from the Extreme Moons. This extraordinary costume had been produced from somewhere in the depths of the Palace of Law, and he was assured that some such garb—and usually more elaborate than this—was expected of anyone speaking directly to the lady Poet Jacinth. The intent was, of course, that his splendor should convey a compliment to the Poet; he only wished that his inner confidence matched his outer magnificence.

Another student appeared in the door, smiling, and indicated that Coyote should follow him. They went down a long hall, turned left and went down yet another, and stopped in a smaller room, octagonal, paneled in wood and smelling of subtle incense. At each of the eight sides there was an oval window, and the student indicated to Coyote that he should go look out.

"Are you allowed to speak to me, Citizen?" Coyote asked the boy abruptly, and was answered by a polite negative shake of the head. He looked at the narrow "student" stripes on the boy's brown tunic; there were three. Apparently this young man was of too high a level to be excused from the rule of speaking only in verse, and not skillful enough to convert the Abban verse to Panglish.

"I thank you, then," said Coyote. "This is the Trance Cloister?"

Another nod.

"I will wait until the Poet has finished her meditation, since she is expecting me. She will come through here afterwards, I take it?"

Another nod, and he was gone. Coyote snorted. Good riddance. How the hell was the business of a Profession, even a religious Profession, to be carried on when people were forbidden to speak except in rhymed couplets?

He went to one of the windows and looked out into the garden of the Trance Cloister. It was oval, like the windows densely green, set with pools and fountains; at the far end there was a circle of great boulders and set within the circle a triangle of gaza trees. Their slender branches were borne almost to the ground with the weight of the huge green star-shaped blooms they carried at this season. In the middle of the triangle he could see the Poet Jacinth, kneeling in a plain robe of scarlet, with her black hair flowing loose down her back. She was motionless, her arms spread to the heavens and her head thrown back, and Coyote fought the impulse to turn and bolt. He felt like a perfumed monkey sent to profane a temple service by a gang of adolescent humorists.

He sent a thought her way, gently, SOMEONE IS HERE, and she turned her head and rose from her knees, looking at him with wide eyes. She hesitated, and then began walking toward him, the scarlet cloth clinging to her in the wind, and he saw that she was very beautiful. Her hair was absolutely straight and fell to her waist like a scarf of black silk, caught back at each temple with a silver clasp. She was deeply tanned, and no wonder, if she spent—as he had been informed—six hours of each day in meditation in that garden. It was a classical face, with high, abruptly slanted cheekbones, a perfect oval shape, an aristocratic nose, black eyebrows like wings, and a slender mouth with a flawless curve. Almost too perfect a face, for his taste; he liked a bit of difference, some flaw to break the mask. But her eyes, as she came nearer, made him frown with interest. He reminded himself to find out if she was on any sort of medication; perhaps the famous Permanent Medication so beloved as a punishment from the Women's Discipline Unit? The eyes were black and enormous, the almond shape praised in old poems, with a violent line around the pupil, and they were so wide open that she looked like a startled animal ready for flight.

She came in through a door at the side of the room and reached out her hands in a gesture that he supposed must be a traditional greeting, though he had not seen it before. He did not touch her, but waited, and when she sank gracefully to the bare floor, her hands folded inside her long, full sleeves, he followed suit and sat facing her. Whatever code of etiquette might apply here, she would not expect him to be flawless at it; he would do the best he could.

She smiled at him, and then spoke slowly, in heavily accented but charming Panglish.

"It is my pleasure that you visit me; so few distractions come to fill my days. And days and nights alike are long when one is all alone."

Coyote considered the speech carefully. Probably, if she had confined herself to the prescribed couplets, he could have followed her, although he did not know the special vocabularies of Poetry. But he was glad no one had told her, because she must be translating the rhymed Abban into English blank verse, a sort of virtuoso performance that he could take pleasure in. There was a pause, a hesitation with closed eyes, before she spoke, but so brief as to be almost unnoticeable. It must take considerable skill.

"Thank you, Citizeness," he said. "If I can offer you welcome distraction I will be honored. But even more important, I come to attempt to insure your safety."

The wide eyes opened wider. The effect was almost frightening.

"Can you tell me, please, my lady Poet, about this poison that they are tormenting you with?"

She closed her eyes for a moment and then looked at him again, solemnly.

"Each morning when I go into the garden, and always when the moon has touched the trees, the poison comes—like knives within my skull—and drives me to the earth, and pins me there. The pain comes again and again, till I feel no more . . . each stab no more than seconds long, but deathly deep."

"Where is the pain?" he asked her. "Can you tell me *exactly* where you feel it?"

"But I have told you once—inside my head!"

"Never cramps in your muscles, or stomach pain—always just stabs of pain in the head?"

She nodded, still smiling, watching him like a child, waiting for miracles.

He thought for a moment. He knew no poison that could behave as this one was supposed to, but then he knew very little about poisons.

"Citizeness?" he asked tentatively. "Is it forbidden for a man to enter the garden where all this happens, once you are there?"

"If you are a man, the keys unlock all doors," she said. "Be at my side, if you will, and welcome there."

She had understood at once, and he was pleased with her.

"That's exactly what's needed," he said with approval. "I need to hear you when the poison takes effect, then perhaps I will be better able to judge. At the moment I'm mystified."

She lowered the disturbing eyes, looking down at her knees.

"If you fail, my friend, I go joyously to death," she said. "If not, I will carry this burden yet a while."

He wanted to reach out, touch her, reassure her, but the memory of the staring eyes kept him back where the rigid, foolish etiquette could not have. The more he sat near her the more he felt that what he saw in her eyes was perhaps not the effect of drugs alone but of some subtle warping of the mind as well, some trace of the ancient sickness they called "madness." He would have to ask if a doctor could be brought to her; in this day and age it was barbaric to find a woman suffering a plague out of the Dark Ages of the twentieth century.

He took leave of the Poet, asking that she arrange for his return visit that night, and waited while she summoned another student to lead him back out to his waiting flier. There was just time for him to have his dinner, make sure that the two women who shared his quarters would not be punished for his neglect in the morning, and then it would be time to come back.

When he lay between Aletha and Josepha, his duties suitably discharged, he asked them about the Poet Jacinth's condition.

"Could she have a doctor?" he asked.

The girls looked at him, amazed, and Josepha spoke to him wonderingly. "Is she sick, Citizen?"

"I think so; I am afraid so. Could she have one?"

"Of course," said Josepha. "She is given the tenderest of care, always. She is beloved of all of us. You must tell them at the Trance Cloister that she is not well, and they will send a specialist at once."

Coyote sighed. "Well, that at least is a relief. I thought it might be difficult . . . and she's pathetic."

Josepha leaned on one elbow and turned to him the inevitable interested face of one woman hearing of another's physical ruin.

"You are not speaking now of the effect of the poison?" she asked.

"No . . . there is something else."

"What is the matter with her, then, Citizen? Could you tell?"

"I think she is mad," he said flatly. "I'm no expert, but it seems to me there is madness in her eyes."

"Madness?"

Aletha spoke then, in Abban, too rapidly for him to understand, and both women laughed softly, turning their heads away. In order not to offend him with their noise, he supposed.

"What's so funny?" he demanded. "Madness isn't funny at all, it's a disease, and a damned unpleasant one. Do you know what it is?"

"Yes, Citizen," they answered respectfully.

"Then why is it funny? Just because the mad don't bleed or break out in spots doesn't mean they aren't suffering."

"Citizen—"

"Yes. Aletha?"

"We would not contradict the Citizen, lowly women that we are."

"Contradict me. I don't find you lowly at all. I find you highly."

"Highly?"

"Highly attractive. Highly pleasant. Highly intelligent. Highly to be recommended."

It was a lie, but he had an obligation to these two helpless hunks of flesh entrusted to his whims.

"Highly lovable," he added, for good measure. He *could* have loved them, too, in exactly the same way Ratha loved her dog. Not one iota's difference.

They were still hesitant, so he coaxed them. When he got back home he was going to say something so outrageous to Tzana Kai that she would hit him for it, just to get the bad taste out of his mouth.

"Please," he said gently. "Tell me. I really want to know why you reacted that way."

Aletha, the braver of the two, sat up and crossed her legs neatly and folded her hands in what he now knew to be the standard posture for respectful discourse.

"Her madness is known, Citizen," he said. "The Poet Jacinth would, of course, be mad. And you must not wish to take her madness from her. That would be very cruel."

"I don't understand."

"Perhaps the Citizen has not taken thought," murmured Josepha.

"Perhaps the Citizen is stupid," said Coyote. "Please explain."

"Think of the way she lives," said Aletha. "She rises each morning at four, and for two hours she must meditate in the Cloister. Then she receives the sick; because she is holy, she can heal where doctors have failed."

"How does she heal?"

"With poetry, of course, how else?"

"Go on."

"That takes her morning, usually. Then she must spend

several hours more in meditation. Then two hours at her official duties—preparing poems for state occasions, for officials who have need of sacred lines to ease the burden of their work, many things of that kind."

"When does she eat, for the Light's sake?"

"Once a day, at the evening dinner hour. Then into the garden for more meditation."

Coyote made a sound of disgust. "And her friends? When does she see them? When——"

"She has no friends," said Aletha. "She is a holy woman, thus she cannot have females for friends. And of course no woman can be the friend of a man; the female brain is not fit for such a role."

"That is not true," said Coyote, raising a mental finger at the Fish and his warnings.

"But it is," said Aletha serenely. "I would not contradict the Citizen, of course, but things are as I describe them."

"As you describe them?"

"The Poet Jacinth cannot have friends; it is forbidden."

"That's not what I meant," said Coyote, but she looked at him blankly and went on, and he gave it up.

"Her madness, under the circumstances, is a necessity."

"Part of her professional qualifications, in short," said Coyote.

"Yes, Citizen. You have understood in spite of the inadequacy of our explanations."

"May she read? Look at threedies? Play a musical instrument? Pick flowers? Swim? What is she allowed to do? When does she have time off for herself?"

Aletha looked shocked and Josepha made distressed noises.

"A holy Poet of the Seventh Level," said Aletha, "even if by the will of the Light that Poet should be a female, has no need of such things, Citizen."

"She summons madness instead."

"Yes, Citizen. It is expected."

"Tell me," said Coyote, "if she were a man, instead of a woman, would she still need madness to support her?"

Aletha laughed and lay down beside him once again, while Josepha went to prepare his bath.

"Of course not," said Aletha. "If a man is Poet of the Seventh Level, his concubines see to it that he is happy. It's not the same thing at all."

94

"And why has she no male concubines?" Coyote demanded.

At the very mention of such heresy, Aletha leaped from the bed and scuttled after Josepha, leaving him to fume alone.

Chapter 7

Coyote sat in the darkness of the gaza trees, where a low chair had been placed for his comfort, and waited for something to happen. Abba's twin moons had just risen and were flooding the garden with their pale green light so that everything seemed edged and stippled with silver-green. The trees stood out in the moonlight like silhouettes cut from paper, no depth to them, like scenery trees for children's plays. The air was thick with the smell of flowers and the wind off the river. From inside the cloister he could hear the sounds of thumb-pianos and small bells, ringing under the tireless hands of the meditating students.

The Poet went to her accustomed place within the circle of great stones, and raised her face to the skies, lifting her arms and spreading them wide. He had watched her the night before; she had stood motionless there for hours, sometimes moving her lips in words he could not hear, sometimes silent. And nothing had happened. No poison. No pain. He was here again tonight to see if it would be different.

He was sure that no one could possibly have come over the walls or down from any of the trees to do her harm, even if it were possible to do so without her noticing—which was not unthinkable in view of the depth of her trance. The moonlight was bright, though, so bright that no smallest movement could go unnoticed. And he was in no trance, except that of boredom.

The minutes crept, one after another. Coyote was tired,

as well as bored. He caught himself wishing there would be another attack on the Poet so that he could get on with this, and was mildly astonished at his own callousness. However, it was possible that his presence here was sufficient to keep whoever was out to harm Jacinth from trying it again, and in that case what would he do? He could not sit here every night from now on, like the guardian angels of prehistory. Eventually he would have to go back to Mars-Central, heavy taxes or no heavy taxes.

The moons rose higher, their brilliance almost blinding. He could easily have read by their light, if he had dared bring anything to read. The poet still yearned toward the sky, not the smallest fraction of her body moving except the ends of her hair streaming in the wind from time to time, and her lips that murmured mysteries. The eyes were always wide; he was sure she had not blinked them once, and he marveled that she could stare into the face of those burning moons . . .

When it happened at last it was so sudden that he was caught by surprise. She dropped without a sound to the grass and lay there, eyes finally closed, mouth wide in a silent scream, her back arched like a bow in her torment. For an instant she relaxed, moaned softly, and then as the pain struck her again she was once more twisted into an arch of agony.

Coyote ran toward her, caught her up in his arms, feeling the spasms of the muscles reacting against the pain, and carried her toward the trees to lay her down. At once, when he passed the border of the circle of stones, she relaxed, and he realized that she had lost consciousness.

He laid her down under the trees, examined her briefly to be sure that she was in no immediate danger, and went quickly back to the spot where he had seen her fall. There might be something there, some clue, something that would give him at least an indication of where to look. Poisons did not simply come out of the air and strike their victims to the earth, not even on a planet where crime was an honorable profession—although, come to think of it, perhaps that was a thought. A dart? A hypodermic from a gun? Both were certainly more plausible

97

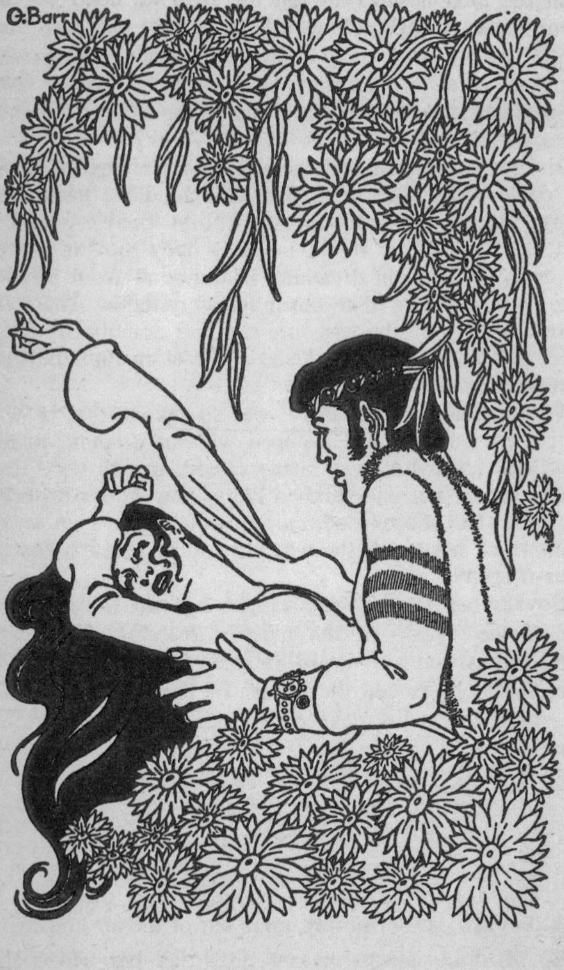
G.Barr

than the undetectable poison in the food! He hurried, pleased with this new idea.

He stood where Jacinth had stood and looked around him, then knelt to examine the grass under his feet, and when the pain lanced through his skull he cried out in astonishment. Caught off guard, he almost activated the shields that would have protected him against the attack, but he recovered enough of his balance to realize that shielding would at once give away to the attacker the fact that someone else was standing in Jacinth's spot, and someone who knew a bit more about what was going on than she did. Instead of shielding he stepped out of the circle; as he had suspected, there was no repetition of the pain. He went back to Jacinth's usual place; immediately the hot knife slashed through his mind, and he moved away again. Again it stopped as he left the circle of stones.

Poison, indeed! He was breathing hard, as much in rage as from the effects of the pain. He went to where he had laid the woman and found her resting, but conscious, smiling up at him, her smile tired but aware, and free of pain.

"My lady Poet," he said softly, "I think we have found the answer to your problem."

She opened her mouth to speak, but he laid his fingers across her lips.

"Don't try to talk," he said. "I am going to carry you into the Cloister and send for your servingwoman to stay with you. When you feel entirely yourself again, we will talk. In the meantime, there is no problem about protecting you against the animal that's after you—just stay out of the circle of stones. You're not required by your office to meditate only in that spot, are you?"

She shook her head, and he nodded approvingly.

"Good," he said. "Stay away from those stones and nothing will happen to you, at least not until it is discovered that you have changed your place of meditation. It would be best if you moved to a different spot each night until we have settled this ugly thing."

He lifted her in his arms and carried her across the garden, indifferent to whether or not such contact was forbidden to her. The extent to which she had been neglected sickened him; obviously no one had bothered to stand close to her at the time of the attacks, but had simply watched from the comfort of the Cloister. If anyone had been with her, any one of the members of the Profession of Law—surely they were at least minimally trained?—any one of them should have known at once that it was not poison but a psi-weapon that was being used against their Poet.

He saw her safely resting in comfort, with a steaming drink beside her and a servingwoman to watch her in case she should need anything, before he left her. He made sure that his instructions about her nightly change of place for meditation were known to someone who would not forget, even if she did, and then he set out to walk back to his rooms, refusing the offer of transport the Poets made him and sending his own flier back empty.

"I'm too angry to ride," he said to them bluntly. "If I walk all the way back to the Palace of Law I may be fit to face another human being by the time I get there."

"And the Poet Jacinth——"

"Take care of her!" he bellowed at them, his patience exhausted. "She has suffered only because you have not prevented it, you versifying fools! Keep her away from that spot in the garden that I showed you, see that she does not always go to the same spot and present herself as a target, and I will see what I can do! Naturally nothing can be done tonight; the Citizen realizes that the hour of accomplishing anything has passed!"

They made no further effort to interfere with him, and he went out into the night to walk off his rage.

When he explained the situation to the proper official the next day he got the response he expected.

"But that is impossible," said the Abban.

"Citizen ban-Drakl," said Coyote wearily, "I'm sorry. Impossible or not, it is so. There is no poison involved in this case at all, as you would have found out for yourself if you had gone to the, pardon the expression, scene of the crime. The Poet Jacinth is being subjected to psi-probe of an impressive intensity, projected at considerable distance."

"How can this be?"

"What do you mean, how can it be? It simply *is*."

"But it is against the law!"

Coyote regarded him carefully and thought for a moment, then shook his head.

"How?" he said finally. "You tell me what that means to you—it is against the law. I see no evidence of any law here on Abba, Citizen ban-Drakl, unless perhaps as applied to the status of your women."

Ban-Drakl made an astonished face. "Perhaps the Citizen has suffered a slip of the tongue?" he wondered. "Is this not the Palace of Law itself?"

"This," said Coyote, "is the Palace of Rules and Regulations. There can be no law—and no justice, my friend—in a society where any law may be broken as long as the proper form has been filled out first. That system prevailed on old Earth for centuries, and came very near bringing about the destruction of the human race on that planet. It works no better now than it ever did."

"The Citizen it overwrought," murmured the Abban politely, and Coyote shrugged.

"I am not here to argue philosophies with you," he said. "Let us drop this discussion, Lawyer ban-Drakl, and take up the problem of locating the individual who wants to destroy the Poet Jacinth. I am as aware as you that the use of psi-probe as a weapon is against the law. It is against intergalactic law as well as Abban, my friend. Nonetheless, someone is doing it, and doing it well. Your Poet could not survive many more such attacks."

To Coyote's amazement the Abban proceeded to pull out a heavy file marked "Current Registered Crimes" and look painstakingly through it.

"No such crime is registered," he said at last. "Shocking. Just shocking."

"The crime or its unregistered status?"

"What, Citizen?"

"Our shock will not help the Poet Jacinth," Coyote went on, ignoring the question. "Have you any idea who might be doing this thing?"

"The Citizen must allow me a moment to think," said the Abban, and Coyote sat back to wait.

"Citizen Jones?"

"Yes?"

"You say this attack is of great intensity, great force?"

"Correct."

"Then it is not something that could be done by just anyone?"

"Oh, no. It would require a real expert, someone of unusual ability and strength, a psi-adept with extensive training."

"All such persons are registered, throughout the Three Galaxies," mused ban-Drakl.

"Right," said Coyote. "And do you know how many of them there are, by any chance?"

"No—do you?"

"Exactly four hundred and thirty-six. Each one was registered with Mars-Central at birth and is employed in some official function for which his abilities specifically fit him. Some are Communipaths, some are in Multiversities . . ."

And some, he thought but carefully did not say, some are TGIS agents.

"You know that all our Criminals on Abba are psi-trained," said ban-Drakl. "Is there any chance that it might be one of them?"

"You mean someone with ordinary psi-talent and a year or two of training?" asked Coyote, thinking of Neo. "Is that the extent of it?"

"Yes," said ban-Drakl. "Could one of them do it—that is, assuming one of them would be so depraved as to commit such a crime, and unregistered, too?"

Coyote shook his head.

"No," he answered, "this isn't on that scale at all. One of your criminals might be able to cause a moderate headache at ten paces, nothing more."

"I see," said the Abban. "I see."

"Good. I am pleased to hear it."

"The Citizen is angry."

"The Citizen bloody well is. This is inexcusable, you know."

"Mmmm. The publicity will not do Abba any good."

"That's right, my friend. It may cut into your tourist trade quite a bit. Psi-probers are not exactly the favored culture-heroes of the citizens of the Tri-Galactic Federation."

"Oh, dear," sighed Lawyer ban-Drakl.

"Oh, dear," mimicked Coyote. "What do you expect to accomplish by sighing and dear-dearing, Citizen?"

"Nothing at all," said the Abban with sudden briskness.

"We must do something specific. What would you suggest?"

"First of all, we notify Mars-Central of the situation and have them check the location and activities of the four hundred and thirty-six people we mentioned. Second, we have one of the Communipaths check those same four hundred and thirty-six to see if one of them is lying."

"They will permit that?"

"If a psi-adept refuses to allow examination by a Communipath, then he has something to hide," said Coyote. "His refusal is as revealing as an admission of guilt."

"I see."

"Then," Coyote went on, "when we find—as I'm sure we will—that none of our known adepts is involved in this filthy business, we set all the Communipaths scanning the galaxies in search of a rogue."

"Rogue?"

"A rogue telepath," said Coyote, "someone who has by some freak managed to keep secret the psi-powers that he has, and is misusing them against others."

"This can happen?"

"It has, on at least one previous occasion; that time it was a baby. But babies don't go around psi-proving people."

"What if they don't find anyone?"

"There has to be a source," Coyote chided. "Psi-probes don't grow like flowers, or fall like rain, Citizen. They come from human minds. And any source of sufficient power to do what this one is doing will be detectable by the Communipaths."

"What if he's shielded?"

"It could be a woman, you know," Coyote said, watching ban-Drakl. The Abban recoiled, as he had known he would, and Coyote scored one point for his side.

"He—or she—" he went on, "cannot simultaneously maintain shields and initiate an attack. The instant the shields are dropped to allow projection of the probe, the Communipaths will be able to locate the source."

"That means the Poet Jacinth must undergo more of this pain? But that is very unfortunate!"

"What is unfortunate," said Coyote carefully, "is that I am prohibited by law—a *real* law this time, from a planet where crime is not conducted like a business—from wringing your unfortunate neck."

"Perhaps the Citizen will explain?"

"There is no necessity whatsoever for the Poet Jacinth undergoing anything at all, can't you see that? Whoever this psi-criminal is, he or she is not sufficiently skilled to select an individual as a target. The projection is being done by visualization of the particular place where the Poet is known to go each night to meditate, and whether there is anyone there in that spot to undergo the attack is not something the criminal knows, probably. Certainly, anyone at all could stand there in her place and provide the proper feedback of pain."

"The attack is simply blind projection, then?"

"Exactly. It will probably be some time—if no one shoots off his big mouth—before it becomes known that the Poet Jacinth no longer goes each evening to that ring of stones in the garden of the Trance Cloister. For as long as that is the case the attacks will probably continue, just as if the Poet were there. It would be a good idea to issue daily reports of her sufferings . . . no, I take that back. Since we can't be sure it will be every night we mustn't do that, we might give the whole thing away. We need vague rumors, only. And the Poet will be quite safe, but the Communipaths will be able to scan for the source of the probe."

"I see," said the Abban again. He saw a great deal, once it had been clearly pointed out to him; it would have been more useful if he had been able to see something by himself.

"Can you take care of the details of all this?" asked Coyote.

"Notifying Mars-Central, asking for Communipath scanning, all of that? Of course, Citizen Jones. It will be done at once. You need not concern yourself further about it."

Coyote stood up. "Very good, then," he said. "I'll go back to my rooms and make my report to Mars-Central."

Chapter 8

FILE 1143.01.b, Segment 2
TOPIC: Rogue Telepath (presumed)
FROM: Office of the Director
Communipath Data and Detail
GALCENTRAL, STATION 7
TO: Lawyer ban-Drakl
Palace of Law
Alsabaid, the planet Abba
DATE: Octoberninth, 3028

1. Thorough checking of the 436 known psi-adepts within the area of the Three Galaxies reveals that each is engaged in the performance of activities known to the Communipath Bureau and fully approved. In those cases where deviancies were found they were personal matters and in no way connected with this situation; therefore no report will be made on them.
2. Extensive scanning of the Tri-Galactic area to its farthest perimeters has as yet revealed no evidence whatever, REPEAT NO EVIDENCE WHATEVER, of any rogue psi-activity emanating from any single source. It is felt that this alternative can safely be eliminated from consideration.
3. Communipaths scanning in the area of the planet Abba itself, however, have located the probable source of the psi-activity directed toward the Poet

Jacinth ban-harihn. The coordinates of said source indicate that it is to be found in that section of the city of Alsabaid known as the "Ruby Ring"—that is, in the Vice Quarter. It was not possible for the Communipaths to locate the source more precisely because of the difficulties with the signal (see below for explanation), but the Vice Quarter is small enough that further investigation by the agent on the spot should not be difficult. Another agent could of course be sent out to assist Citizen Jones in this investigation; however, since intergalactic distance is irrelevant to the Communipaths' efficiency, it is felt unlikely that there is anything that could be done there in the way of psi-scanning that has not already been done by them. (Coordinates will be found below.)

4. It should be noted that the Communipaths report that the signal itself coming from the psi-source in the Ruby Ring is aberrant in some way that they are not able to specify. As is well known, the psi-voice of any given individual, rather than being recognizable by sound as is the overt voice, is usually identified by such factors as a specific taste, smell, appearance, and the like, which is perceived by the individual receiving the telepathic projection of the voice. The Communipaths state that this particular signal is so muddy and distorted and full of static that they find it impossible to describe in any significant way. They feel that this fact may be of the utmost significance for the investigating agent, since it indicates that the source is not one of the usual ones with which we are accustomed to deal.

5. If the difficulty in handling this situation persists, Communipath Bureau (Data and Detail Division) should be notified in order that further action may be discussed. In writing, please refer to above file number.

END OF REPORT

PS: This signal is really weird, friends . . . it tastes like chocolate/peanut butter/fish/cactus-fruit/seaweed/lake-spice/casserole, and it smells like everything it doesn't taste like. We wish you luck and would like to know what the character putting it out is like.

Andy Maryn

Coyote read the report through carefully, then handed it back to the Lawyer.

"That's clear," he said. "I'll go down to the Ruby Ring this evening at the proper time for the attack to take place, and see what I can find."

Ban-Drakl cleared his throat. "I seem to recall, Citizen, that the last time you went to the Ruby Ring there was some sort of unpleasantness."

"Oh, that," said Coyote blandly, "that was quite all right. Just some of your honorable Criminals playing their little registered games, no?"

"The Citizen would make us very unhappy if he fell once again into participation in these games to which we are referring."

"Don't worry," said Coyote. "I'll have my interpreter along with me this time. He'll be careful—he wouldn't dare let me get into trouble."

"That will be a load off our minds," said ban-Drakl. "We have grown fond of you, Citizen."

Coyote refused to answer that. He left with dispatch and went to brief his interpreter, who seemed perfectly calm about the whole thing.

"See here, ban-Dell," Coyote asked him, "are you sure we can get through this evening without my ending up maimed in some way? Otherwise I'm going to demand a police force to go with us."

Citizen ban-Dell was a small man and a chubby one, but he had great dignity. "There is no occasion for alarm," he assured Coyote. "I am not to be tricked so easily as all that."

"Good," said Coyote. "Very good. Because I am. I am to be tricked more easily than you can imagine."

If ban-Dell felt that that was a strange thing for an intergalactic agent to say he carefully suppressed his opinion.

They arrived at the Ruby Ring just as the moons were rising, since all the known attacks had occurred shortly after moonrise. Coyote wore the gray robe that almost let him pass as a man of Business; his interpreter scuttled protectively beside him.

"Where shall we begin?" ban-Dell asked, putting on hand on Coyote's arm. "We can't just prowl the Ring at random."

Coyote shrugged. "You're the expert, you know, a native of this society. What would be *your* suggestion?"

"Well . . . there are two possibilities. Since this crime is unregistered it is being committed either by an amateur or by a real expert. That is, our criminal is going to be at one of the extreme ends of the scale, not some average person in the middle."

"Not Citizen Joe Criminal, you mean."

"I beg your pardon?"

"Where would we look for one of these extreme ends, Citizen ban-Dell?"

"That's hard to say."

"You must have some ideas."

It was, of course, the case that if Coyote could get within fifteen feet, roughly, of the attacker, he would be aware of him. His psi-bilities were adequate for that. But the Ruby Ring covered a very large area compared with the fifteen feet that represented his maximum receptive range.

The little man bit his lip and frowned.

"I think," he said, "that we might save some time if we went first to the Kalif."

Coyote raised his eyebrows.

"The term," said ban-Dell, "is borrowed from old Earth culture, I believe. Some kind of an official. When our culture was . . . er . . . adjusted to suit the requirements of the Tri-Galactic Federation, the gentleman from Mars-Central who helped us with the adjustments made us quite a list of such terms. The Criminals took a fancy to 'Kalif.' "

"What is his function, exactly?"

"He's a sort of administrator, coordinates all the activities . . . you could accurately say that he does the same thing for the Criminals that our Chief of Legislators does for the members of Law, except that of course the Kalif's authority does not extend beyond the limits of his own profession."

"By all means, let's go see him. Where do we find him?"

The Abban pointed to a street sign above their heads. It was shield-shaped and made of a scintillant lavender material, and it bore a plain legend. The Panglish equivalent was "Street of the Kalif."

"Follow me," said ban-Dell.

They crossed the street, brushing off, as they went, the Criminals who stepped up to them with an extraordinary variety of propositions, and headed down the Street of the Kalif. Half a block, and Coyote was standing in a state of total awestruck delight before the Palace of Crime.

He was simply going to have to get over this culture-bind that kept him associating crime with the furtive, the secret, and the squalid, he thought. If anything, the Palace of Crime was even more magnificent than the Palace of Law; it was a full city block of archways, and balconies, and gardens, and hanging vines, and winding staircases. The architects had apparently, must have, worked directly and with meticulous fidelity from the illustrations of an expensive edition of the *Arabian Nights*.

"Are those real woods and real tiles?" Coyote marveled.

"Oh, no," said ban-Dell. "That would have been rather ostentatious, don't you think? The construction materials are synthetics. But I find them extremely convincing, don't you?"

"Indeed I do," said Coyote. "I would have taken them for the real thing."

They were ushered into the offices of the Kalif of Crime after a number of subordinates had expressed their great pleasure at seeing with their own eyes a high-ranking agent of a Tri-Galactic anticrime organization. Some of the Criminals ran down corridors and brought back little groups of others to marvel at him, and Coyote tried unsuccessfully to ignore the wondering murmur of Abban that seemed to follow and surround him.

"Why, exactly," he demanded under his breath, "are they so amazed at the sight of a TGIS agent?"

"Well . . . we are a practical people, you know."

"So I've heard."

"What strikes them as so incredible is that governments would go to the expense of an organization like TGIS instead of simply incorporating crime into their own political structure. As we do here. They find you an example of off-world extravagance, unheard-of luxury, and decadent waste."

"They don't realize that their taxes help pay for TGIS?"

"Of course not. Why should they?"

When you are as accustomed as Coyote was to being considered an unfortunate and regrettable necessity, the idea that you are instead the priceless toy of a society that can afford to spare no expense is something of a shock. Coyote followed ban-Dell into the Kalif's office without another word.

The Kalif greeted them expansively, listened to their description of their problem with attentive nods, and then stretched out his delicate long hands to express his surprise.

"Such a terrible thing," he mourned, "such a dreadful thing. And within my own territory! I can hardly bring myself to believe it—are you quite sure?"

"You Excellency," said Coyote, hoping that was the right title, "if I were to ask you where your com-set is, would you have any difficulty in telling me?"

"Of course not, Citizen. I see it right here, at the left side of my desk."

"Well, for a Communipath the location of a psi-source is just as simple. They perceive its location just as surely as you do your belongings. It can't be a mistake."

"Citizen ban-Dell?" said the Kalif. "Do you verify all this?"

"I do, Your Excellency," said ban-Dell. "I know very little about the Communipath system, except to be grateful that they are able to serve as a communications network for the galaxies and spare us waiting centuries between the question sent and its answer. But Citizen Jones is an expert on this subject; he remembers, for example, when the life expectancy of a Communipath was only eighteen years."

"There was such a deplorable condition as that?"

"Until very recently," said Coyote, feeling ancient, "and reform is only just beginning."

The Kalif clucked his tongue in distaste. "And I hear

you Inner Galaxy people criticize *our* political system! Amazing!"

Coyote stared at his feet, determined not to rise to this sort of baiting. All he needed to thoroughly foul up this evening's work was to become involved in a political debate with the chief Criminal of Abba.

The interpreter put in a tactful word. "Can you help us in any way, Citizen Kalif?"

Citizen Kalif! thought Coyote. He hadn't expected that.

"Hmmmm . . ." said the Kalif. "Let me think . . . certainly I know of no one who would do a thing like this. On the other hand, I know everyone who is within the area of the Ruby Ring, I know what each one of them will and will not do, and I have assistants who are experts on each and every activity carried on in the Ring. If I call them all in and we all put our heads together, I see no reason why we should not come up with some answers."

IF WE ALL PUT OUR HEADS TOGETHER!

It was like an electric shock. Coyote sat there, stunned. He was remembering, as a child, the training in the Communipath Creche on Mars-Central. The matrons had had them all sit on the floor in a circle, with their foreheads touching, and they had played games, trying to guess which one was thinking, trying to touch each other's thoughts. That was it. It had to be.

He stood up abruptly and both Abbans looked at him with polite surprise.

"I know who's doing it," he said wearily. "I should have known the first night I was here, if I hadn't been so wrapped up in that red herring about poison. Damn it all! I must be getting old."

"Well, tell us, Citizen!" the Kalif exclaimed.

"It's very simple, and it was you that gave me the information."

"I did."

"You did. We should all put our heads together, you said. And then I remembered. The first night I was here, when I was wandering around the Ring in the clutches of your estimable poisoner, Neo what's-his-name . . ."

"Ban-Valdevere," murmured the Kalif.

"Ban-Valdevere? Really?"

Coyote blinked and went on.

"Anyway, we went down a kind of alley, and through a

111

window I saw this circle of people, sitting on the floor with their heads touching, all of them chanting . . . Neo said it was a religious cult. I haven't thought of it since."

"Of course!" The Kalif struck his desk with his fist. "You say the Communipaths complained that the signal was muddled!"

"Exactly. And that's what you would expect, under the circumstances. None of those people could project across a dining table by themselves, but by all sitting close together and concentrating on a single image, night after night, they are able to amplify their individual weak signals into a single strong one."

"Amazing," marveled the Kalif. "I will have to be very stern with them."

"You know who they are, then?"

"Certainly. The cult of the Holy United Mind. I'm as bad as you are, Citizen Jones; I should have known at once, if only from the stupid name they chose to give themselves."

"Well, then!" said the interpreter, standing up to join Coyote. "Let's go deal with this matter at once. It should be a matter of routine, now that we know what's going on."

Coyote shook his head. "No," he said. "I know exactly what should be done about this, and I'll handle it myself. And it can't be done tonight, it's too late. Tomorrow night I'll come back and put a stop to their dangerous little game for good. In my own way."

"You realize that we cannot allow you to do them harm, Citizen?" the Kalif put in. "TGIS or no TGIS——"

Coyote stopped him with a gesture.

"Don't worry," he said. "Not only won't I harm them, I'll provide them with the peak religious experience of their lives. I'll come get you both and take you with me to watch, and if at any moment you feel some of their precious rights are being violated, you can interfere, okay? Fair enough?"

"Fair enough," said the Kalif. "I look forward to the demonstration."

Then he clapped his hands and a subordinate entered.

"I want to show our friends around the Ruby Ring personally," the Kalif said cheerfully. "Summon a thaan-carriage at once and call ahead to all my favorite places—tell them to expect us and to make ready."

He looked at Coyote and winked, a long, slow, experienced, evil wink.

"I think you're really going to like this," he beamed.

Chapter 9

Coyote was impatient the next day, as well as suffering slightly from the effects of the previous night's tour with the head man from Crime. He told the women good-bye, effusively enough so that they would not jump to the conclusion that he was in some mysterious way displeased with them, and went out to walk through the streets of Alsabaid.

There were women on the street, moving along in twos and threes, heavily veiled and covered by shapeless, full, flowing robes in colorful patterns. Thaan-carriages were everywhere, and mobs of students on their way to their classes. The city was beautiful; Coyote felt better just from looking around him.

He went into a park where a display of mobile flowers was whirling solemnly around a fountain, and sat down on a bench to watch the flowers and the pale green water leaping in the sunshine. The flower leading the dance was an enormous specimen, almost five feet tall, with diamond-shaped petals of a gold so pure it hurt the eyes, and great sawtoothed leaves perhaps six inches in length. He wondered where it came from, and then saw the tag on one of its leaves—Alepha 238. Coyote whistled softly . . . that was a long way from Abba.

A small bell rang at his ear, and he jumped. It the air beside his head there hung a small star-shaped bauble, repeating the same bell sound at intervals of ten seconds or so and evidently a constructed, rather than a natural, phenomenon. He looked around him at the other citizens enjoying the fountains, and noted that none of them seemed at all alarmed by this pretty toy that had appeared so suddenly in their midst.

"Citizen," he said to the man closest to him, a burly gentleman in the white robe with dark blue stripe that marked him for a Scientist, "can you tell me what that thing is?"

"That thing?"

Coyote pointed.

"Oh, yes," said the Scientist, "you mean the Memo Star?"

"Memo Star . . . I am an off-worlder, Citizen. Could you explain?"

"Assuredly, Citizen. I would be honored. The Memo Star is attuned to any given citizen's registration number—"

"What registration number?"

"On your Federation credit disk, Citizen."

"Oh, yes. I'm sorry."

"Quite all right. As I was saying, the Memo Star is attuned to your personal number and can be sent after you to convey messages. Yours must have something rather private to say to you."

"Why do you say that, Citizen?"

"Because it hasn't given you your message. If it were only some business appointment, or a message that one of your sons wished to speak to you, something of that kind, it would simply make that announcement by your ear and return to the sender."

"Ah," said Coyote, pulling his beard. "Interesting. Well, then, how do I go about getting it to divulge this private message it has for me?"

The Abban pointed toward a small egg-shaped structure down one of the paths in the park where the fountains were.

"That is a privacy booth, Citizen," he said courteously. "Take the Memo Star with you and go into the booth. There you will find a star-shaped projection on the wall. Touch the Memo Star to the projection and it will deliver your message."

"Thank you, Citizen," said Coyote, "you are most kind."

"Not at all," smiled the Citizen. "I am honored."

Coyote reached out cautiously and plucked the star out of the air, still chiming at him. It did not burn him or shock him or sting him, and he made his way to the privacy booth. Presumably, since the Abban had not worn the robes of a Criminal, he was safe in following his instructions; he went into the booth, located the star-shaped stud on its wall, touched the Memo Star to it, and waited.

At once the little bell rang again, and then the Star spoke to him in a tinny, mechanical voice.

"The Poet Jacinth sends you her best wishes," it said, "and asks that you come to her tonight at the seventh hour. She will send her servingwoman to the west entrance of the Trance Cloister to guide you. End of message."

Not sure that he had heard properly, Coyote touched the little gadget to the wall stud again and listened to the message a second time. There was no mistake. But what could the lady Poet want? He was willing to go, but he was *not* going to get dressed up in the monkey suit again. She would see him in his own clothing or she would not see him at all.

He went back out, carrying the Star, which promptly took off and disappeared from sight. He nodded at the questioning look of the Abban Scientist, to indicate that he and the trinket had managed without difficulty, and began to walk.

Could the Poet Jacinth perhaps have some information on the psi-attacker that they did not have? It seemed very unlikely. Or was she simply requesting a report from him on the progress of the investigation? Her days were so fully occupied with her duties that the evening meeting she had specified was not surprising, and if she did not keep him long he would still be able to reach the Ruby Ring soon after moonrise.

His curiosity was aroused. He went to find a shop where he could buy her some little gift to take along with him. Finding something suitable would help to pass the time.

When he finally sat before her, not in the anteroom this time, but in another, smaller room that he supposed must be her own, he handed her the gift that he had chosen. It was a small scroll of synthosilk, bearing a delicate drawing of gaza trees blowing in the breeze. He saw that she was pleased, and accepted her thanks, glad that he had chosen something she could enjoy.

"Now," he said, "what can I do for you, my lady Poet? I will be happy to do anything I can."

She hesitated for a moment, and then spoke, slowly, in her oddly accented Panglish.

"I would dispense with the speech of Poetry for this one evening," she said carefully, "if you would not find it offensive."

"Why should I?" asked Coyote, surprised and touched. "You must speak however you want to speak."

"Then I will speak as any women to any man," she said. "The fashion of poetry alone in my speech is only of meaning if you are a man of Abba . . . I ask your patience, I am clumsy."

Coyote waited, and when he saw that she was also waiting he spoke again.

"What is it, Citizeness? Did you want me for some particular purpose? The investigation is going well, you should be safe from the psi-attack after tonight, if that is worrying you."

She shook her head.

"There is another burden, Citizen, of which you might ease me, if you were willing."

"You have only to tell me," said Coyote. "If it is within my power, I will do it gladly."

"It is difficult."

"Try," he coaxed, gently.

"At the age of twelve," she said slowly, "I was brought here from my father's house. Since then, to the limits of my poor ability, I have served the Holy Light. Through all that time I have written poems of every kind, the poems of love as well, but I have never known love, Citizen. No man of Abba dares touch a woman who is a Poet."

Coyote was silent, unable to think of a single suitable thing to say.

"Citizen Jones," she said, "I am weary of my condition. Will you help a poor woman of Abba?"

Coyote stared at her, not quite certain that he understood, but very much afraid that he did. She looked back at him, unwaveringly.

"I have never seen such huge eyes as you have, Citizeness," he said softly, playing for time.

"That is because each day a liquid is dropped in them—so that I am able to look at the twin moons without harm.

"Will you help me, Citizen?" she asked him again. "They say that I am mad, but I would not hurt you."

Coyote considered the matter. Even allowing for the difference in cultures, there didn't seem to be any way he could misinterpret what she was saying. The lady desired to be deflowered and felt he was the proper agent of that defloration.

Just what, he wondered, might be the diplomatic repercussions if he complied? Would he find himself legally her husband, for example, by Abban law? Or would he be guilty of an "unregistered" crime? He was reasonaly sure he had too much diplomatic immunity to be in any serious danger, but it could get very unpleasant, and the Fish would get a kick out of letting him stew in an Abban jail.

"Would you give me a moment?" he asked, finally. "I'll come back at once." He bolted from the room with as much haste as seemed possible when he took into consideration Jacinth's feelings. He found a student and demanded a Memo Star, with instructions for its use.

When it came back to him ten minutes later, and he took it into a cubicle meant for other functions, to listen to it, he was satisfied. The interpreter had made the answer quite clear.

"By all means take the Poet to bed," the return message said. "We've always wished someone would, because it would be certain to improve her poetry, but none of us could possibly have managed it, not with her being Poet and woman at one and the same. We would be honored, Citizen Jones."

There was no getting out of it, then. Coyote went back to Jacinth's room, whistling softly under his breath, and went to find her still sitting as he had left her, waiting for his answer.

She looked up at he came in, and smiled sadly.

"I have offended you, Citizen," she said. "I ask your forgiveness; a woman does not always know what is best to do."

"Hush," said Coyote. "I can think of nothing I would rather do than love you. I just had some business that had to be settled first."

He reached out and gathered her up, carried her over to her narrow bed, and laid her down.

"You are always carrying me," she laughed.

Coyote chuckled. "The Citizen is honored," he said.

"I am very frightened."

He touched her hair gently. "Don't be," he said. "I have never had any complaints yet."

Tenderly he removed the scarlet tunic that covered her small, perfect breasts, the breasts of a young girl, and the untouched flaring curve of her loins. He was so involved with her beauty, and with the rush of desire that he felt at the sight of her, naked but for the black hair that flowed about her like silk, that he thought of nothing else. Certainly not of the Palace of Crime, and the men who waited for him there.

She cried out once, softly, as he entered her, and he gentled her tenderly with his hand.

"That's all the pain that there will be, love," he said to her. "That's all there is; from now on it should be only joy."

He hoped so. It mattered deeply to him that this first— and possibly last, for her—lovemaking should be something she could look back upon with happiness rather than regret. He settled to the grateful task of pleasing her, to making all things one for her, knowing that the chances of bringing her to climax were very slim but determined that she should at least find pleasure, and was rewarded finally by the high cry of perfect ecstasy that he would not have dared promise her.

Afterward she fell asleep in his arms, and the moons were high in the sky before he could bring himself to lay her aside, put on his gray cloak, and make his way to the Palace of Law.

Chapter 10

"You're sure," said the head of the Criminal Profession as the three of them made their way to the meeting place of the cult called Holy United Mind, "you're absolutely sure that there's nothing in your plan that will harm any of these people?"

"You have my word," said Coyote. "Am I to understand that you don't consider that a sufficient guarantee?"

"The Citizen is justifiably annoyed," murmured the Abban. "I withdraw my question."

Coyote looked as offended as possible, glaring straight ahead of him and pulling at his beard.

"We are almost there," put in the interpreter hastily. "What do you want us to do?"

"Just stay by the windows so you can see the fun," Coyote said, "and don't interfere."

"Where will you be?"

"I'm going around the other side and come in through that little door there on the right. All you have to do is wait here and watch."

He left them there and slipped around to the other side of the room where the cultists were crouched uncomfortably with their heads pressed together. Beside the door he shucked his long robe and gave his costume a last look to be sure it was satisfactory.

It was certainly unusual. He wore a skin-tight suit of brilliant scarlet and a hood of synthetic golden feathers with silver tips and flecks. Wings of the same splendor trailed from his shoulders almost to the ground, looped up and fastened to his wrists so that when he raised his arms he looked amazingly birdlike. Giant birdlike. Carefully scattered all over the scarlet skin-stocking were small pinhead-size mirrors; they were of no use now, but later they would be indispensable to the effect he intended to create. Lightning bolts were going to issue from them, for example, and some very fancy rainbows. Whatever his inspiration dictated.

He'd used this costume twice before and it always did the job. He rarely went on an assignment without it, taking it along as a matter of course, along with a couple of others of slightly different design but equal magnificence. This one had been carefully prepared by the TGIS psychologists to combine half a dozen ancient archetype figures, with a heavy saturation of Angel/Devil. Coyote rather fancied himself in it, and regretted the fact that he was unable to see it in its full splendor, since he was immune to his own illusions.

He prepared a careful image, also prescribed by the psychology staff. Clouds of smoke, booming thunder, tongues of flame, and all the little mirrors activated. He imagined himself surrounded by a seething maelstrom of noise and turmoil and tumultuous color, and when he had the whole thing visualized he projected it at sufficient strength to blanket the room ahead of him, and walked in, straight into the center of the chanting circle.

The effect was all that he had hoped it would be. The cultists were paralyzed with fear and with the "DO NOT MOVE FROM YOUR PLACE, YOU SINFUL SCUM" instructions that they were getting from Coyote along with the fancy stage props. As one man, they prostrated themselves before him and peered at him through trembling fingers from flat on their bellies on the floor.

"Shame!" he thundered, projecting each word as he uttered it, although that was probably not necessary. He believed in being absolutely sure.

"A POX UPON YOUR HOUSES! MAY YOUR WINDOWS CAVE IN AND YOUR DOORS CRUMBLE ABOUT YOU! MAY YOUR BEDS CATCH FIRE AND BE CONSUMED IN FLAME! MAY ALL YOUR SONS BE IMPOTENT AND YOUR DAUGHTERS INCURABLY CROSS-EYED! MAY YOUR LIVESTOCK DIE,

MAY YOUR FLIERS ALWAYS BE BROKEN DOWN! MAY YOUR WOMEN RISE UP AND REBEL AGAINST YOU AND SHAME YOUR HOUSEHOLDS! MAY YOUR CHILDREN CURSE YOU TO YOUR FACE AND YOUR SERVANTS THROW THEMSELVES INTO THE RIVERS RATHER THAN REMAIN WITH YOU IN YOUR DISGRACE! MAY YOUR HOMES FALL IN ABOUT YOU AND SUFFOCATE YOU IN THEIR RUBBLE! MAY THE VERY HILLS OF ABBA MOVE TO COVER YOUR SHAME!"

The men began to wail, begging for mercy, pleading their innocence. Coyote knew what they were seeing. A giant creature, far larger than a man, garbed in lightning and rainbows, winged like a bird, around whom swirled colored mists and jets of flame. No wonder they were scared. He would have been, too.

"I AM OFFENDED!" he bellowed. "GRIEVOUSLY HAVE YOU OFFENDED THE HOLY LIGHT AND ME, ITS SACRED MESSENGER! HOW DARE YOU MOVE TO HARM THE HOLY WOMAN JACINTH, CHOSEN POET, CHOSEN VOICE OF THE HOLY AND ALMIGHTY LIGHT? SCUM! SWINE!"

He took a deep breath and upped the output of lightning, putting it out now not only in the standard natural yellow but in poisonous greens and purples as well. He wreathed his golden head with a whirling circle of hissing snakes.

"ONLY IN ONE WAY CAN YOU SAVE YOUR SHAMEFUL SOULS! I AM COME TO SPARE YOU ETERNAL DAMNATION, SENT BY THE HOLY LIGHT, IN INFINITE MERCY, TO OFFER YOU AN OPPORTUNITY TO ESCAPE THE JUST PUNISHMENT THAT YOU SO HEARTILY DESERVE! DOGS! PIGS!" And he added the ultimate insult . . . "WOMEN!"

They were utterly destroyed, he noted with satisfaction. It wasn't even a challenge, it was so easy. But then he should have expected that; if they hadn't been pretty piss-poor they wouldn't have been in this idiot cult anyway.

He let them grovel and beg a while, stepping up to the local color that filled the three-foot area in the center of which he stood, and then he told them.

"YOU ARE TO CEASE YOUR PERSECUTION OF THE POET JACINTH."

They would.

"YOU ARE TO KNOW THAT SHE IS HOLY, THAT SHE IS BELOVED OF THE HOLY LIGHT, THAT NOT ONE OF YOU HERE IS FIT TO KISS HER SLENDER FEET."

Yes, yes. They knew that now.

"HENCEFORTH IT IS YOUR SOLEMN TRUST TO DEVOTE YOURSELF TO THE GLORIFICATION OF THE POET JACINTH, AS BEFITS HER HIGH STATION. YOU WILL MEDITATE UPON HER BEAUTY. YOU WILL COMPOSE HYMNS TO HER MAGNIFICENCE, TO HER TOTAL PERFECTION, TO HER UNSPOTTED SUPERBNESS."

They would do that, they assured him in unison. They would, they would! If he only would go away and allow them to begin.

"NOT UNTIL I AM CERTAIN THAT YOU HAVE UNDERSTOOD WHAT YOUR FUNCTION IS TO BE HENCEFORTH, MISERABLE DOGS!" he shouted at them. "NOT UNTIL EVERY LAST ONE OF YOU HAS CONVINCED ME THAT HIS LIFE, FROM THIS MOMENT ON, WILL BE DEVOTED TO THE GLORIFICATION AND THE WORSHIP OF THE LADY POET JACINTH, BELOVED OF THE HOLY LIGHT, WILL I LEAVE THIS ROOM OR REMIT THE CURSE THAT HANGS OVER YOU!"

He did quite a lot of that stuff. The more he did of it the more he enjoyed it, as a matter of fact. He threw in some restrictions and some ritual and half a dozen embryo prayers based upon careful review of half a dozen assorted guaranteed "holy" books from a number of planets. He told them what kind of flowers they were to put in the bouquets they sent the lady Poet, what kind of incense to burn. He even added a sacred day of feasting and celebration, to be held in Jacinth's honor each and every year. He saw no reason why she should not get all the mileage possible out of this, after the suffering these idiots had caused her.

It was so satisfying that he hated to quit, particularly since he was only just beginning to really hit his stride. But he knew what would happen if he didn't stop. He'd get carried away and overdo it. There'd be a great religious revolution sweeping Abba, with no foundation whatsoever except the visions he'd laid on these poor groveling specimens. There'd be protests from the Abban government, hysteria from the officials of the already extant churches, offended heavy taxpayers, the Light knew what else. Generalized hell to pay.

He settled for a last threat of what would happen to them if they did not obey this holy vision they'd been so fortunate as to share, the threat involving their foreskins, their testicles, and their pubic hair, and then disappeared in a cloud of purple and orange smoke.

He made it out the door, collapsed the wings, pulled his gray cloak on over the rest of it—just remembering to pull off the golden feathered hood as he started outside—and then hurried to where the Abbans were waiting for him. He was anxious to have their reactions to all this. They should have been pleased, he felt. After all, no one had been hurt, the story of the punishing messenger would spread and serve as a significant deterrent to any like misuse of psi-power, and the new cult of Jacinth-Glorification should keep a lot of otherwise bored misfits happy, busy, and out of trouble.

It was not until he had almost fallen over them, where they knelt on the sidewalk moaning and shivering, that he remembered. He shouldn't have let them watch. And not just them. There were two other converts to the new sub-religion, citizens who had just happened to wander by during his performance.

He leaned against the building and ticked off a list on his fingers. First. Convince the two innocent bystanders that nothing had happened. Second. Convince the Chief of Crime, and the interpreter, that nothing had happened. Third. *Tell* the last two what had happened, once they were free of the mystical experience he'd just shoved down their heads.

It took him a while.

He had in fact been away only nine weeks, and apparently Tzana had not missed him at all. He noted that fact with great pleasure, and sat down and watched her at her work. As he sat he amused himself by sending a series of elaborate projected insults her way.

"What's the matter with you, Coyote, have you lost your not overly impressive mind?" she demanded finally, her hands on her hips and her words fairly spitting sparks. "May I suggest that you go play Super-Telepath somewhere people don't have any work to do? There are some children down there in the park, I noticed them as I came in; why don't you go down and play with them? They'll probably let you be It!"

Coyote grinned at her.

"Well? Did you come all the way over here just to pick a fight?"

"No, blessing," he said cheerfully, "I'm just trying to get the nasty taste out of my mouth and head."

"What nasty taste?"

"The nasty taste of subservient women!" he crooned. "Nasty, foolish, docile, subjugated, subservient women, with no minds of their own, and no thoughts to put in them if they had any! The Light be praised, I'm back here once again with you, just as you are—obnoxious, arrogant, pigheaded, overbearing——"

Tzana was a telepath of no mean projective power herself, and she almost tore his head off before he could get his shields into action. A little stunned, he reached out and took her in his arms.

"Thank you, love," he murmured, holding her tight, "I really needed that. . . ."

Epilogue

MODULATION IN ALL THINGS

1

The young man in the student tunic motioned the emissary to be seated on a low wooden bench against the wall. The bench was the only furnishing the room contained except an altar in the center and a high case of ancient books.

"Please be seated," he said, "and when the Poet Jacinth has ended her meditation I will come and take you to her."

"You are allowed to speak to me in prose?" marveled the emissary.

"Certain Poets serving in the function of communicators between the Temple of Poetry and the people are excused from the vow of verse-speaking while on duty, Citizen," murmured the student.

"Very good. And you'll go with me to see this . . . this Poet?"

"Yes, Citizen."

"The Light be praised," said the emissary with satisfaction. "I wasn't happy about going by myself."

The student nodded to show his understanding. "One's first interview with the Poet Jacinth is not an experience to be taken lightly."

"Do you know her well?"

"I? Certainly not! She is female, and not of my household."

The emissary stared at the floor. "I see," he said. "I am sorry to have offended you, young Citizen."

"It's perfectly understandable," said the student gravely. "There are no traditions available to our people for dealing with a Poet of the Seventh Level who happens, the Light alone knows why, to be female."

"It hardly seems possible, even after all these years."

"And yet," said the student, "she has given our Temple the finest poems of this age. The Light does not err, you see."

"She is expecting me, of course?" asked the emissary.

The student frowned and studied his fingernails. "There was a messenger from the Council this morning," he said. "However, the Poet Jacinth has been in meditation since before dawn; there has been no opportunity for the messenger to communicate with her."

"What! You mean to tell me, man, that I must see her without any advance preparation whatsoever? Surely *she* is allowed to speak only verse?"

"Correct, Citizen ban-Dan."

"Then how am I—how are we to communicate?"

"I would suggest that you instruct the Poet Jacinth merely to listen, Citizen. That would be less complicated."

"What," breathed the emissary, "are they trying to do to me? What are they trying to *do?*"

The student chuckled softly. "Apparently," he said with a sly casualness, "the Council acted rather hastily on this question."

He was gone before the hot words that leaped to the emissary's lips could be spoken, and it was thoroughly apparent that Citizen ban-Dan's elaborate costume and impressive title had not impressed the student in the least. It was, of course, quite possible that the youth was the son of a wealthy family and accustomed to elaborate dress and ceremony. One could not tell with students, since they must all dress alike until graduation, regardless of their rank or the circumstances of their households.

There was therefore nothing left to do but wait and hope that he would do and say the right thing, and that the Poet Jacinth would see him soon, before he died of the heat.

The student erred, though, mused Citizen Arafiel ban-Dan, Emissary Extraordinary of the Legislative Council of the Planet of Abba. The Council had not acted hastily. The formal carrying out of the decision had perhaps been rather abrupt, but it had required three days of angry debate in the Council Hall before all the members had been convinced that it was really necessary—or for that matter, seemly—to disturb the Poet Jacinth with this problem.

Some of the Elder Members had been almost apoplectic with rage at the very idea. Indeed, the Member from the Sector of the Lion, a conservative and wealthy sector inhabited mostly by the old and sedate families of Abba's very rich, had threatened to retire from the Council if the others persisted in their intention.

"I say it is blasphemous!" he had shouted, his old voice trembling but still powerful. "Never in the history of Abba, never once in ten thousand years, has a female been involved in matters of government—that is the first thing! And even if the Poet Jacinth were not a female, even if that did not enter into this, the very idea, the very concept, of approaching a Poet of the Seventh Level, a holy being dedicated to a life of meditation and sacred composition, and asking that Poet to assist in a . . . a translation! Gentlemen, my gorge rises at the thought! On two counts, this whole plan is both blasphemous and obscene, and I will take the Sector of the Lion out of Abba if necessary before I will see it implemented by this Council!"

The emissary chuckled, remembering the old man's thunder and fire, ringing through the hall and all being duly noted by the robosecs on their aluminum pedestals. Nothing bothered *them*, of course, except noises that interfered with the performance of their duty.

It had been far from easy to persuade the old man— and many others who, though perhaps less dramatically vocal, sided with him on the question. It *was* a tricky problem, an unheard-of problem, with no precedent to follow, and a planet with ten thousand years of recorded history is accustomed to a heavy backlog of precedent.

Fortunately, they had had a powerful weapon on their side. The Elder Member from the Sector of the Lion was a wealthy man, and it was his credit disk that was being hurt by the situation that they wanted the Poet Jacinth to solve for them. Had it been anything else he would never have given in.

They had shown him the figures, patiently repeating, until he at last grasped the size of the sum that it was costing the planet of Abba—and the taxpayers of Abba, including himself as one of the heaviest-paying of those taxpayers—to provide the ten planet-colonies of Abba with enough edible protein to maintain their populations. They had reminded him, also, of the inevitable tragedy that faced Abba if the planet-colonies could not be made more economical to operate, to provide living-space for the ever-growing population that threatened to swamp the home-planet. They had shown him the bill that resulted from attempting to ship food out from Earth, the agricultural planet two galaxies away. And they had waved under his nose, finally, all the incredible advantages of that ubiquitous plant from the distant world X513, the *ithu* plant that was 93 percent edible protein, and that would grow anywhere, anywhere at all.

The old man had gasped and stuttered and spluttered, but in the end he had given in and the rest with him.

And now here he sat, Emissary of the August Council, all decked out in title and finery to cover the trembling man beneath, all alone with the task of justifying all this to the holy woman.

The Emissary sighed a mighty sigh. He was not a devout man. Religion, he felt, was a necessity, since it kept the females busy and out of trouble, and since it provided the Three Galaxies with those very useful people, the Maklunites, with their insane dedication to service and self-sacrifice. It was not for men, however, particularly busy men like himself. It was only at moments like this that he felt its lack. He gave the altar across from him an uneasy look, wondering, and then put the unworthy thought from his mind. After all, this was but a female he was to deal with.

When at last he was allowed to enter the garden of the Trance Cloister he found the Poet Jacinth sitting on a boulder underneath a small waterfall, waiting for him to speak. He stood before her, miserable, torn between his proper knowledge of the proper attitude to take when speaking with a female and the proper attitude to take when speaking with a Poet—never mind a Poet of the Seventh Level!—and she had smiled at him and nodded pleasantly and put him at ease with a casual couplet on the weather, and he had simply thrown tradition to the winds, since it failed him here, and begun to speak.

"I come to you today on a strange errand, my lady Poet," he began. "It would perhaps be easier for both of us if you would hear me out before you speak."

She nodded, her lovely face solemn and attentive, leaning forward slightly to hear him better. It was most flattering. She reminded him of one of the youngest and most delightful of his concubines, and he warmed slightly to his task.

"You will know, of course," he said, "of the ten planet-colonies maintained by Abba. They are planet-surrogates, of course, artificial asteroids except for three that were once this planet's moons. On all of these ten planets, Poet Jacinth, there is a very serious problem, and it is the opinion of the Council that only you can help us find its solution."

She frowned, the perfect brows drawing together charmingly over her dark eyes, but she had remained silent as he had asked her to do. It crossed his mind that she was after all only a young female, and a virgin, and that it was not going so badly.

The Emissary relaxed, and if he had been watching Jacinth he would have seen a smile tug at the corners of her mouth, but he was staring at the blossoms of the gaza trees and trying to keep his mind on the seriousness of his mission, and he did not notice the Poet's lack of respect.

"You see," he went on, "the living-space on these ten colony planets is desperately needed by our people. The crowding in our cities in such that, given the culture of our people, we cannot continue to support our population. You understand, of course, that the extended household of the family, with women's quarters and parks and garden, could not lend itself to blocks of buildings hundreds of stories high?"

She nodded charmingly.

"We must then send colonists, pioneers, to the new planets. And it is quite true that people, particularly the young people, and most particularly those young people who have not managed to win a place in any of the Professions except that of Service, are eager and willing to go as colonists.

"Unfortunately, most unfortunately, however, the colonies are not succeeding." A gaza blossom, a great green star covered with white pollen, fell onto his robe, and he brushed it off impatiently.

"Where was I?"

To his great pleasure, the Poet clapped her hands softly, and immediately a student appeared with a tray of teas and wine, giving him a moment to recollect himself.

"Ah, yes," he said, as the student poured their drinks, "the colonies are failing. They are failing because on not one of the ten planets within the practical reach of our starships can any of the protein plants, which we know of, be successfully cultivated. This leaves us with three choices. One, we can send edible protein, grown on Abba, to the colonies; this we are now doing, but we are no longer able to bear the drain on our own resources. Two, we can send protein from Earth, at an incredible and unendurable cost; this would not help much longer even if we could afford it, since almost all of Earth is now given over to fruits and vegetables. Third, protein synthesis can be instituted by the colonists themselves. This, too, is being done, but with the best facilities available to our scientists, it has been impossible to devise any sort of synthetic protein that can be eaten with pleasure over any long period of time. The colonists rebel against the diet, they find it tasteless and boring, and the eventual result, if they force themselves to eat it for the sake of the colony, is an epidemic of psychosomatic stomach difficulties—all in their heads, certainly, but quite as destructive to their health as genuine organic disease. We have been at our wit's ends, my lady Poet—until we learned, two years ago, of the existence of a protein plant which is both good to eat and economical to grow, and which can be grown on the ten colonies . . . or anywhere else, for that matter."

He glanced at his ring, saw with horror that there was little time left before the compulsory Hour of Meditation. He would have to get through the rest of it in a rush.

"This plant," he said, "comes from the world X513, whose inhabitants are known as the Serpent People. We need only establish communication with them, only learn how trade may be discussed! It is that simple—and this we have not been able to do. The greatest linguists of Abba have put two years of work into the attempt to learn this language, and they have failed. In every conversational attempt made so far, the Serpent People have left after only a few sentences, obviously deeply offended in some way, and it has only been with great difficulty that we have managed to obtain their consent to one more meeting, two months away, at the Intergalactic Trade Fair. They do not come to the Trade Fair ordinarily . . . they are a curious, proud people, apparently quite self-sufficient on their world, not at all anxious to engage in any social or business activity. We do not understand them, and they either do not understand us or do not care to try."

She was nodding gravely, her eyes lowered, one hand idly playing in the falling water behind her.

"Poet Jacinth," he said earnestly, "the future of the colonies, and therefore the future of this planet, depends upon you. You are the greatest expert in language and the use of language that we have. There is no one else we can turn to now to determine how the language of the Serpent People can be used successfully. It is for this reason alone that we have interrupted your solitude and your meditation. We hope that you will appreciate the gravity of the situation. We hope you will forgive us."

He had come to an end at last, and he realized, ashamed, that he was trembling and covered with perspiration. There he stood in his almost-royal garments, he, a male of the Profession of Government, trembling like a frightened child before a slender little female in a red linen shift. It had been too much for him; never in his lifetime had he so exposed himself before a female, not even before his mother. He *had* bolted then, as he had wanted to do at the beginning, thrusting into her hands the packet of language tapes and the translations of the experts, and had almost run for the exit gate. There had been no time for her to speak, nor would he have waited to hear her if there had. His only concern was to escape, to get out of his borrowed finery and into his own clothing, and to spend at least half an evening in the company of his most humble and unintelligent concubine. He did not even know if he had succeeded or failed in his mission, nor did he care; he had done all that he could do.

II

Jacinth went over the data for the third time, wonderingly. The linguists, all Poets of the Fourth Level, had done what appeared to her to be an excellent job. They had taken standard tapes beamed from X513, submitted them to computer analysis in the ordinary way, and seemingly had produced all the needed information. And yet it had not sufficed for communication.

Methodically she went over it again, one infopacket at a time. The answer had to be in there somewhere.

They had isolated and catalogued the consonant phonemes first. M, B, V, TH, Z, L, R, NG. Only eight? Two nasals, two liquids, two fricative, and two stops. That wasn't much to make a language of, eight consonant phonemes. And only eight vowels as well, three nasals plus the standard five, A, E, I, O, U. A sixteen-phoneme system did not offer much complexity of sound, unless it was a tonal system, and the computer had ruled that out. It was a non-tonal.

Morphemes appeared to be all of one syllable, all simple in construction. It looked like a language constructed by a child, or an extremely language-naïve adult. It was curious that it should have offered difficulty at all, much less that it had stumped the best of their linguists for two years.

The Poet Jacinth wished, not for the first time, that she had someone to talk to. As a fully invested Poet, however, she was required to speak only in verse, and it did very badly for general discussion. Plus, she was not allowed to speak to females, lest she give them unseemly ideas of aspiring to the Profession themselves. And males did not care to talk to her because of the conflict between the attitude of paternal tolerance due her as a female and the attitude of humble reverence due her as a Poet.

She sighed and went to the corner of the room where her com-system console stood, and punched the key for a servorobot. When it appeared she requested a small computer and a linguistics program tape.

She attached the computer hook-up to her com-system, folded her slim legs under her, and sank down at the keyboard to work.

REVIEW LINGUISTICS PROGRAM, she tapped out.

In a moment the computer clicked and its side panel flashed the single word COMPLETED.

She then inserted the tapes prepared by the linguists for the language of X513, instructing the computer to indicate deviations from the basic information on the first tape.

While the computer hummed its way through the task she examined once again the threedy image of a citizen of X513 that had been included with the data, marveling at the beauty of the being whose picture glowed in her hand.

She inserted the threedy slide in her com-system and punched the PROJECT button, and at once the image was projected lifesize in the center of the room for her examination.

These were a very beautiful people, if the specimen whose image she saw before her was any example. It stood perhaps eight feet high, if "stood" was the proper word to use, since the Serpent People resembled a serpent more than any other creature with which Jacinth was familiar, and their manner of "standing" was much that of the King Cobra of Earth. How much length might be involved in the coiled body she could not judge, but eight feet was held upright. The entire body was transparent, except for what she assumed was the head, and appeared to be made of strung beads of translucent crystal, caught together at the top and twisted into a rope. Alternate strands of the "beads" were in shades of deep green and blue, the others were without color, and the whole meshed at the top in a sphere of opaque beads which must house the being's brain and whatever structures it might use for speech.

She studied it silently, knowing very well how deeply she might be in error in her analysis even of its physical structure. Perhaps the seeming "head" was really the creature's foot, or its stomach, or its sexual organs. Perhaps it was not one being but a colony, each strand representing a unique individual, all joined in some communal lifesystem. There was as yet no way of knowing, since no citizen of X513 had ever been examined by the Doctors of Abba, or of any other planet so far as was known.

Behind her the computer clicked again to signal completion of the review. She turned off the slide and went to examine the side panel. It said NO DEVIATIONS.

Very well, then. Her instinct had found no flaws in the analysis. Her computer agreed with her instinct. Therefore there *were* no flaws in the analysis, the translations of the language were as correct as could be asked, the representations of the sounds on the tapes were adequate, and no portion of the system violated the base theory of universal linguistics. Nonetheless, it had not been possible to speak to the Serpent People.

The Poet Jacinth smiled; it was a stimulating problem.

Somewhere in all of this there had to be the reason, the single explanatory factor that was being overlooked.

She left everything as it was so that she might return to it when she chose, deactivating the servorobots that would otherwise have put everything away for her, and went out into the garden.

Sitting on her favorite stone, the soft sound of falling water on her back, she closed her eyes and performed the ritual seventeen breaths, allowing all consciousness of her surroundings to leave her. When her relaxation of consciousness was complete, all that was left to her of physical awareness was the sensation that both the light and the water flowed through her being as freely as through the air, and she waited, patient and poised. Somewhere, there was something that she almost knew, something that she almost realized, something that was familiar about the language and about the problem, something that she remembered, almost. . . . She let the time pass, unaware, and waited.

And then she had it. She allowed her consciousness to return to her gently, becoming aware of the garden about her, noticing that it had grown almost dark and the air in the garden had turned cold and heavy with pale green dew. There would be people upset about her.

She rose quickly and went into her room, gathered up the materials and reactivated the servorobots, and then she began to dictate, ignoring the soft bell that called her to eat. She would eat when she had finished with this, after she was sure that she had captured all that she must say, before she became in any way confused. She began to dictate to the com-system, watching with pleasure the intricate pattern of its dancing lights as it wrote down her words:

TO THE COUNCIL OF ABBA:

When first I read the letters that you sent me
(and I am honored that you asked my help,
for in the service of this spinning world
lies my whole happiness and my satisfaction)

there came to me a sense that I had known,
somewhere before, a problem of this kind,
a feeling that I once solved just such a problem,
as a child, perhaps? Certainly long ago.
And so I went at once into my garden
and let the Light direct me to your aid.

Then I remembered what I had forgotten.
I was a child, a small and noisy female,
spending my days in the courts of my lady mother,
and there had been summoned to the household ban-harihn
a student of Poetry, ranking at Third Level,
whose single function was to teach us all to sing,
and some were to learn to play the singing strings.
And so ...

The members of the Council were hushed as it came to an end. It was, somehow, blasphemous that a female should write so well; it was humiliating that she should solve a problem that had baffled the greatest of their linguists; it was embarrassing that the solution should have been so—once pointed out—overpoweringly obvious.

Emissary ban-Dan stepped to the center of the Council Chamber and cleared his throat.

"Is it clear to all the Members," he asked, "just what the Poet Jacinth is telling us? I should like to add that her conclusions have, of course, already been checked by the linguists and she is quite correct. There should be no further problem in our communicating—after a fashion—with the people of X513."

"But how is it possible," demanded a Member, "how is it possible to speak such a language?"

The Emissary tried to think of some tactful way to put his answer, but there didn't seem to be one.

"You are familiar with the colorful birds of Old Earth. ... the parrots?" he asked courteously.

"Yes," snapped the Member, "not that I see how that is relevant."

"It is quite, quite relevant. You see, actually we *cannot* speak the language of X513. As members of the human race, our human capacity for language does not allow us to do so, any more than the parrots can speak Abban or

Panglish or any other human language. However—again, like the parrots—we can learn to mimic, and, after a fashion, to communicate. At least to the extent of trade, which is all that we really need, you know."

Several Members were on their feet now, demanding the floor. The Chairman recognized one, who demanded, his voice shaking, if Citizen ban-Dan was insinuating that these people of X513 were superior in intelligence to humans and that we were in effect too *stupid* to speak their language?

"Citizens," said ban-Dan worriedly, hoping the information the linguists had given him would get him through this without disaster, "I have said nothing of the kind. I said to you that their language equipment was *different*. Superiority has nothing to do with it. What reason has there been to believe that an alien race, totally nonhuman, would share the language equipment of humans? What sort of pompous, insular idea is that?"

The Council was silent, and the Emissary drew a deep breath and went on.

"I cannot imagine it, myself," he admitted. "But it nonetheless true that the people of X513—who, by the way, resent being called 'Serpent People' since they are neither serpents nor people—the people of X513 speak their language with no difficulty whatsoever. Their infants speak it flawlessly by the age of three or so, just as do your Abban children. Certainly we of Abba shall not be able to speak it, however, without the aid of some sort of mechanical device."

There was still no comment, and he smiled to himself and went on. "I have here a set of threedies for projection prepared by the linguists. They have been hastily put together and are somewhat rough; I think, though, that they will make everything clear. In fact, I probably need show only the first."

He lifted his hand and on all sides of the Council Chamber a single image was projected. It was a huge circle, divided into eight equal segments, like the ancient dessert called a pie. At the center point of each segment there was a single vowel symbol; at the boundary between each segment, on the outside rim, there was a single consonant; and each segment was numbered.

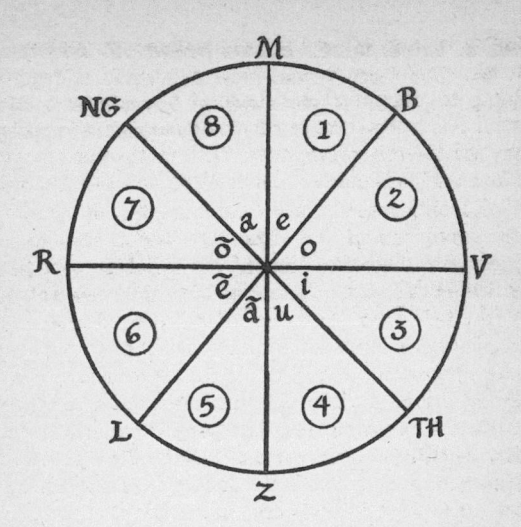

Diagram: A circle divided into 8 numbered sectors. Around the circumference are consonants: M (top), B, V, TH, Z (bottom), L, R, NG. Near the center are vowels: a, e, o, i, u, ã, ẽ, õ. The sectors are numbered 1–8 clockwise starting from upper right.

"This is the whole solution, gentlemen," said the Emissary quietly. "There are, as you can see, only sixteen sound segments in the entire language.

"What the Poet Jacinth remembered was an incident from her childhood. A music teacher had been brought to instruct the women of her household. He had explained to them the manner of playing and singing a simple folksong in the key of A. Then he showed them how to play the same song in the key of E, and again in the key of C. The Poet Jacinth remembered her amazement and her disbelief; it seemed to her at that time that it could not be true that the same song, with the same words and tune, could be played in two different keys. And what struck her even more forcibly was that the same song, played in two different keys at the same time, created an unholy discord. She was so concerned about all this that it was necessary for the music teacher to explain to her the theory of keys and modulations, something that bored the other females of the household to such an extent that the child was punished for her curiosity.

"Citizens, this is a language that modulates; the analogy with music is exact and precise."

The Emissary glanced at his notes, hoping that he would not become as confused in reading aloud the example given him by the linguists as he had become in reading it to himself.

"Refer to the projected chart, if you please," he said. "Now, a given segment, say the syllable represented by the letters MEB—see them there, E at the point of the segment, and M and B at the boundaries—this syllable "meb" meaning roughly "table for eating," will transpose in another environment. For instance, if one says to a servant, 'Set the table for dinner,' the syllable must be rendered VITH, using the letters of the third segment of the circle, the one reserved for speaking to someone of lower status. If, on the other hand, one calls a beloved friend to join one at the table, the word must be pronounced MEB, using segment one of the wheel of letters. In an emergency, if the table was on fire, for example, the word would become THUZ, using segment four. If the table were a work of art, it would be referred to as a LER, using segment six, which is reserved for art and ritual.

"And so it goes, you see—there was nothing wrong with the translations of the words as prepared by our linguists, it's just that the 'word,' for the people of X513, is not a stable unit. It changes constantly, depending upon the social situation, the status of the speakers, and the like."

"Ah, yes," said the senior Member from the Sector of the Fish. "Now I begin to see. Let us say that one of our linguists heard a citizen of X513 referring to a necklace as a BLUB when speaking to an assistant. That would be the proper term for addressing someone of inferior position. Then when our linguist attempted to compliment the X513 person on the fine workmanship of the BLUB he would have addressed *him* as an inferior! No wonder they were offended."

"But surely," commented the Member from the Sector of the Panther-Ram, his beard quivering with indignation, "surely they should have been aware that one could make unintentional errors in a language of such incredible intricacy!"

"Why?" asked the Emissary. "They have no difficulty with their language, nor do they see it as one of incredible intricacy. They had no difficulty avoiding making errors in *our* language, apparently, either—why should they expect us to make errors in theirs?"

"It's utterly incredible," said the president of the Council, wearily. "You realize, I am sure, that the only way we will be able to speak this language is with the help of a computer; certainly we could not follow the modulations quickly enough without such help."

There was an embarrassed murmur through the Council Chamber and, to his horror, the Emissary heard mutterings in the back about the feasibility of applying the same principle to Abban in order to allow a modulation of the language that would be suitable for speech with females. As if life were not complicated enough!

"What we *can* do," the president went on, oblivious to the absurdities in the back of the room, "is have the linguists and computers compose for us an opening speech to be addressed to the people of X513 at the Intergalactic Trade Fair. This must be a speech which will unambiguously explain our linguistic situation to him. This is most important, since presumably once he understands what the problem is he will be more tolerant of our subsequent errors. And," he concluded, "we will have our protein source for the colonies. This is a great day for Abba, Citizens, and one to be long remembered."

Emissary ban-Dan raised his staff of office, requesting permission to speak, and the president nodded gravely.

"Citizen President," said ban-Dan, "what about the Poet Jacinth?"

"What about her? What do you mean?"

"Well, you realize what she has done—she has single-handedly solved the major problem of the future existence of ten planets. It is not as if the people of X513 would have been willing to discuss matters in the intergalactic gesture language, you know. The situation was *really* desperate, and it was the Poet Jacinth who came to our rescue. It seems to me that she should have some sort of reward, some recognition."

"She is a female, Citizen."

"But—"

"She has been signally honored, after all, in being allowed to participate in an activity of our government, something no female has ever done before."

"But—"

"No doubt our own linguists, had they had sufficient time, would have reach the solution without her assistance."

"But, Eminent Citizen, I still feel——"

The president leaned from his chair and shook a warning finger at the Emissary.

"Modulation—that is, *moderation*—in all things, young man! Moderation in all things!"

And he rang the gong to dismiss the Council.

THE END

DAW BOOKS

Do not miss any of the great science fiction from this exciting new paperback publisher!

☐ **THE 1972 ANNUAL WORLD'S BEST SF Edited by Donald A. Wollheim,** and presenting the finest science fiction stories of the year in one great anthology; including Clarke, Sturgeon, Niven, Anderson, etc.
(#UQ1005—95¢)

☐ **THE DAY STAR by Mark S. Geston.** In the sunset of humanity, they set out to reconstruct the glories of Earth's finest hour. (#UQ1006—95¢)

☐ **TO CHALLENGE CHAOS by Brian M. Stableford.** Last trip out to the only planet that spanned the two universes and two opposing laws of physics.
(#UQ1007—95¢)

☐ **THE MINDBLOCKED MAN by Jeff Sutton.** Manhunt in the 22nd Century—with a Solar Empire at stake.
(#UQ1008—95¢)

Four new SF books each month by the best of the SF authors. Ask your favorite local paperback book shop or newsdealer for DAW BOOKS.

DAW BOOKS are presented by the publishers of Signet and Mentor Books, THE NEW AMERICAN LIBRARY, INC.

THE NEW AMERICAN LIBRARY, INC.,
P.O. Box 999, Bergenfield, New Jersey 07621

Please send me the DAW BOOKS I have checked above. I am enclosing $_____(check or money order—no currency or C.O.D.'s). Please include the list price plus 15¢ a copy to cover mailing costs.

Name_____

Address_____

City_____State_____Zip_____
Please allow about 3 weeks for delivery

DAW BOOKS

Do not miss any of the great science fiction from this exciting new paperback publisher!

☐ **SPELL OF THE WITCH WORLD by Andre Norton.** The long-awaited new extra-galactic adventure by America's fastest selling SF author. (#UQ1001—95¢)

☐ **THE MIND BEHIND THE EYE by Joseph Green.** A giant's body is directed by an Earthly genius on an interstellar espionage mission. "A tour de force of the imagination"—Times (#UQ1002—95¢)

☐ **THE PROBABILITY MAN by Brian N. Ball.** The man of a thousand life-roles goes to unravel the secrets of a planet older than our universe. (#UQ1003—95¢)

☐ **THE BOOK OF VAN VOGT by A. E. van Vogt.** A brand new collection of original and never-before anthologized novelettes and tales by this leading SF writer.
(#UQ1004—95¢)

Four new SF books each month by the best of the SF authors. Ask your favorite local paperback book shop or newsdealer for DAW BOOKS.

DAW BOOKS are presented by the publishers of Signet and Mentor Books, THE NEW AMERICAN LIBRARY, INC.

THE NEW AMERICAN LIBRARY, INC.,
P.O. Box 999, Bergenfield, New Jersey 07621

Please send me the DAW BOOKS I have checked above. I am enclosing $_____ (check or money order—no currency or C.O.D.'s). Please include the list price plus 15¢ a copy to cover mailing costs.

Name_____

Address_____

City_____ State_____ Zip_____
Please allow about 3 weeks for delivery